"You're

He scanned the picture Laura presented, starting at her bare feet with toenails painted bright purple. She wore khaki shorts and a matching T-shirt.

He cleared his throat. "I'm sorry. The door to the barn is locked. Can I have the key?"

"Give me a minute and I'll join you. I need to go through my dad's stuff anyway."

Jack shifted his box. He didn't want her invading his space, distracting him. "It's dirty out there, I can handle it."

"What, I can't get dirty?" Laura reached for a key tied to a faded blue ribbon and handed it to him. "I'll meet you in a few minutes."

Jack stood staring at the doorknob, key in hand. It'd been a long time since he'd noticed another woman with interest. It was impossible not to notice Laura Toivo. Losing Joanne had left a gaping hole in his life, but he was finally putting it back together. Building a secure environment for his daughter Angie. He didn't have the time or energy to date.

If only he didn't find tall, blue-eyed blondes attractive…

JENNA MINDEL

Originally from central New York State, Jenna Mindel lives in northwestern Michigan with her husband and their three dogs. She loves activity that's conducive to daydreaming, whether it's walking the woods, picking mushrooms and berries, fall leaf peeping or zipping along nearby snowmobile trails on her Polaris 600 Classic.

Jenna's always been a dreamer. From the time she was a kid, she relished the dashing heroes and feisty heroines found in fairy tales. She completed her first illustrated novel, a romance, in sixth grade.

In a rush to grow up, Jenna graduated high school a year early and went to college in pursuit of a career—changing majors faster than the seasons and forgetting all about her love of story. After marrying her college sweetheart, Jenna landed a job in banking that has spanned more than twenty years and several positions.

In the midst of her corporate climb, Jenna joined Romance Writers of America and her love for romantic stories was reborn. Ten years later in 2001, her first Traditional Regency was published, and in 2006 Jenna became a RITA® Award finalist. But the world of contemporary Christian romance beckoned, and Jenna answered the call to write the books of her heart.

Mending Fences
Jenna Mindel

Steeple
Hill®

Published by Steeple Hill Books™

STEEPLE HILL BOOKS

**Steeple
Hill®**

PLEASE RECYCLE
THIS PRODUCT IS RECYCLABLE

Recycling programs
for this product may
not exist in your area.

ISBN-13: 978-0-373-87576-4

MENDING FENCES

Copyright © 2010 by Jenna Mindel

www.SteepleHill.com

Printed in U.S.A.

"By wisdom a house is built, and through understanding it is established; through knowledge its rooms are filled with rare and beautiful treasures."
—*Proverbs* 24:3–4

In memory of a dear friend, Amber Schalk

Chapter One

Laura Toivo stopped by her assistant's desk before she went home to change. "Cindy, are the reservations for tonight's dinner meeting set for eight o'clock?"

"They are." Cindy, at twenty-six, was five years Laura's junior, but every bit as hungry for success. "Close the Albertson deal and you'll get promoted to senior sales exec."

Laura drummed a pencil against her lips. Everyone knew she'd thrown her name in the hat. She wanted to move up. A promotion might be hers *if* she succeeded. After years of proving herself, it boiled down to the outcome of tonight's meeting. "That's what I'm hoping for."

Closing a deal was the sweetest side of sales. When everything clicked, it was like celebrating a lucrative marriage—one she hoped to make happen with Albertson Manufacturing.

Not that she knew anything about marriage. Once upon a time, she'd longed for a husband, house and kids. But that was before she'd had a taste of domestic life. After a brief engagement fraught with tension due to her fiancé's young daughter, Laura had had enough. Or rather, her fiancé did by breaking it off nine months ago.

Laura scanned her list of cell phone messages. Too many to

follow up on tonight. She rolled her shoulders to stretch out the knot of tension that had become a permanent fixture in the middle of her back. There was only one person she could count on. Herself.

"Laura? Anthony from corporate is on line three," Cindy said.

The knot pulled tighter. Speaking of her ex-fiancé… "I'll take it at my desk."

Stepping into her gunmetal-gray cubicle, Laura slipped off her headset and picked up her phone. "Hey, Anthony."

"I knew you'd be working late." His voice was soft, but carried a hint of regret. Or maybe it was condemnation.

"I heard you've got a big deal going with a plastics company. Keep it up, you're getting noticed."

"Thanks." Laura traced the buttons of her phone with her fingertip.

"I called because…well, I'm getting married."

Laura closed her eyes. He'd set a speed record, even for a rebound relationship.

"Aren't you going to congratulate me?"

"Congratulations." Her well wishes sounded dull. Lifeless.

"She's Brooke's teacher. You'd like her."

Brooke was Anthony's obnoxious seven-year-old. Laura couldn't please the girl no matter what she did or didn't do. Obviously, the kid had bonded with her teacher. So had Anthony.

She spotted her direct line blinking and jumped at the chance to end the sensation of her heart bleeding all over her desk. "I'm happy for you, Anthony, really I am, but I've got another call."

She heard him sigh. How many times had he accused her of putting work first? When he'd made her choose between work and him, work always won. Work didn't hurt her. "Take care, okay?"

"You, too." She connected with the other line. "Laura Toivo."

"Laura, you have to come home, your mother's had a stroke." Her aunt's frantic voice rang through the phone.

"How bad?"

"We don't know yet, honey. She's in ICU. She needs you. We both do."

"I'll be there as soon as I can." Laura stared through the glass partition at Cindy.

Laura had to make that meeting. Her mom was hospitalized, surely a few hours wouldn't change anything. But what if a few hours was all the time her mother had left? She'd regret it the rest of her life if she didn't see her mom one more time.

What if—

Panic coiled in her gut, making Laura sick.

Cindy poked her head into Laura's cubicle. "Everything okay?"

"Call Mr. Albertson and postpone my dinner plans. I've got to go to Michigan. It's my mom—I've got to go home."

It was late when Laura pushed open the door to her mom's hospital room. Stepping closer, she stared at the frail-looking woman lying in a bed surrounded by monitoring machines. The stroke had aged her mother, making her look older than her seventy-four years.

If Laura were a good daughter, she would have visited more often. But she wasn't a good daughter. She was an only child who'd never figured out how to please her mom.

Her mother's eyelids fluttered. "Is that you, Laura?"

"How are you feeling?" Her whisper came out sounding choked.

"My left side is nummmm." Her words slurred. She opened only one eye, the other lid drooping.

"I know." It wasn't easy seeing half her mother's face immobile.

"Have you eaten anything? I can get you something," Laura asked. Did they feed stroke patients?

"Too much trouble." Her mom's thick slur held a trace of stubborn martyrdom.

Laura knew if she went out of her way to bring food, it would sit untouched and uneaten. With a sigh, she peered out the window at the shiny black water of the Portage River. It'd be crammed with boats lapping up the last days of summer come daylight.

"Are you home to stay?"

Laura fiddled with the buckle to her purse. Pressure. Whether she closed a deal, tried to make a relationship work or please her mom, the pressure built and simmered, never finding release. "People depend on me. It's not easy to get away."

"You're too thin."

"I can't cook like you do." Laura pulled a chair closer to the bed. How long did they keep a person with a stroke? She'd left a message for her sales manager that she needed family leave.

"Your hair looks lighter."

"I just had it done." Laura threaded her fingers through her highlighted blond bob. Looking like she hadn't worked hard this summer was a sure sign of success, wasn't it?

After hours of sitting beside her mother, watching her sleep, the door opened. Her mother's only sibling and younger sister, Nelda, entered with a fresh-cut bouquet of flowers in her perfectly manicured hands.

"Good, you're finally here." Aunt Nelda gave Laura one of her pointed glares—as if driving through the night from Wisconsin was not enough. Married to a man who'd once been an actor off Broadway, her aunt dressed like she was headed to Hollywood instead of the local Wal-Mart.

"How's Anna?" Aunt Nelda kissed her sister's forehead.

"A little weak," Laura's mom whispered, her slur worse.

Aunt Nelda pinned Laura with another stern look. "You're lucky your mother and I were shopping in Houghton when she had her stroke. There's no telling what might have happened had she been home *alone.*"

Like she needed more guilt. Laura rubbed her aching head. "I need coffee. Do either of you want anything?"

"I'll meet you in the cafeteria in a few minutes."

Aunt Nelda wanted to talk, but it was a conversation Laura didn't look forward to.

Twenty minutes later, Aunt Nelda sat down across from Laura. "Sweetie, you look beat up."

Laura cradled her mug of coffee and shrugged.

Aunt Nelda patted her arm. "I'm sorry, are you okay?"

"I'm working on it." Laura cringed. She'd sounded too much like her mom.

"How long are you home for?"

"I don't know, a couple weeks?" Laura lived in Madison, Wisconsin. It was six hours south from her mother's hospital room in the Upper Peninsula of Michigan, but it might as well have been halfway across the country.

Aunt Nelda fetched a mug and a fresh carafe of coffee. "What if you need more time?"

Laura stared at nothing in particular.

"Laura," Aunt Nelda scolded softly, "your mother needs you. It's not like she has other kids to lean on. Nancy and I visit when we can, but your mom's going to need constant care."

Laura avoided her aunt's gaze.

"What if you moved back home?"

Laura straightened. "I spent my whole life trying to stay out of Mom's way, get away from the U.P., and make something of myself. Moving back is the last resort."

Aunt Nelda shook her head, making her drop earrings bounce against her neck. "Why?"

"Because I'm on the verge of a big promotion. There's no need to jump to conclusions just yet."

"Strokes at your mother's age are serious, no matter how mild the damage," her aunt whispered.

"What am I supposed to do? Uproot my whole life and make us both miserable? Mom doesn't want me here. She never has."

Aunt Nelda sighed.

"I've suggested she move near me."

Aunt Nelda stirred sugar into her coffee. "Your mother will never leave that house. I know, I've offered for her to live with Ed and me. I'm sorry to be so hard on you, but you're all she's got."

Her cousin Nancy's three young children were no doubt part of the reason Laura's mom wouldn't think of living with Aunt Nelda and Uncle Ed. Her aunt had her hands full watching her grandkids while her divorced daughter worked full-time.

"I could hire someone to come in," Laura said.

"Who's going to pay for that?"

"Me."

"I didn't think you were doing *that* well."

With that promotion…

Laura had homework to do. Her mother's insurance might not cover home visits. She'd have to borrow against her 401K, or maybe her condo. Either way, she'd figure it out.

"What about selling the barn with half the acreage?" Aunt Nelda said.

"Daddy's barn?"

Aunt Nelda brightened, clicking her hot pink fingernails on the table. "Why not? It's not doing anyone any good sitting there empty. You might get a good price for it."

"Do you think Mom will agree?""

"She doesn't have much of a choice." Aunt Nelda rubbed Laura's forearm. "Go home and get some sleep. I'll call my friend who's a Realtor and see what she thinks."

Laura stretched when she stood. Aunt Nelda's idea was a good one. She needed her mom's agreement to make it work, but then real estate didn't move fast in the U.P. They had time. She gave her aunt a kiss on the cheek. "Thanks, Aunt Nelda."

Her aunt looked surprised. "It'll work out, Laura. You'll see."

"You've got to be kidding me!" Jack Stahl threw his hands up with disgust.

"Didn't you get my letter?"

Jack clamped his mouth shut before he said something he'd regret. "No, Carl, no letter."

"I know we agreed for you to rent month by month, but I had to sell the place. My wife took the kids to live with her parents in Saint Ignace. I closed last week."

Their agreement had been verbal, and Jack could have kicked himself. What had he been thinking not to call and confirm his plans? He reached out and squeezed the guy's shoulder. "I'll find another place. I'm sorry about your wife."

"Thanks, man." Carl looked away. "Life stinks, doesn't it?"

"Sometimes." Jack scanned the fields surrounding Carl's house. They were in the middle of nowhere with only a few other homes along the road, and those were miles apart.

"Do you know of any other houses for rent in the area? My daughter, Angie, starts school in a couple of weeks and I'll be working nearby."

Carl shrugged. "There's a real estate office at the corner before you hit town. They might be able to help. They found me a small place just north of here."

"Thanks." Jack collected the boxes he'd left a few months ago—cleaning stuff and a few tools.

He thanked God he'd found out about this situation, before the movers showed up this weekend. A lucky stop after dropping off his son, Ben, at Michigan Tech. The past six months, he'd put his life in order to move. He'd been so sure, and now…

He backed out of the driveway and headed toward his motel room. It was too late to stop by the real estate office. He ran a hand through his hair. Being both mom and dad to his daughter, Angie, was becoming impossible for both of them. He couldn't get anything right.

It'd been a rough couple of years since his wife, Joanne, had died. They might not have had the kind of relationship that inspired love sonnets, but she'd been the ground wire in the family. Joanne had kept them connected, involved in church and the community. Too late, he'd realized how much of his time and attention he'd denied her. Working around the clock to buy into a lucrative vet practice at the expense of his family was a lesson learned too late. He couldn't make up for lost time, but a better future waited.

If he could just find another house.

Jack pulled off the road and rubbed his eyes. It had been so easy with Ben, but he didn't have a clue how to reach his daughter. Forcing this move had pushed her further away.

With a defeated sigh, he bowed his head. "Dear God, I'm in way over my head. Show me where to go from here."

The low hum of locusts and the wind swishing cornstalks in the field next to him was interrupted by a new noise. The grind of a motor sounded in the distance. Looking across the road, Jack spotted an attractive blonde astride a riding lawn mower.

He surveyed the two-story house in need of paint and a hundred feet to the right was a large barn with a stone foundation, also in need of some fixing up. His heart pounded as he stared at the sign posted in the front yard: Barn With Apartment And Twenty Acres For Sale.

Jack got out and walked across the street to get a better look. He tried not to gawk at the woman on the mower, as he signaled with waving arms and then pointed at the sign. He had to know more.

She drove the mower toward him.

Squinting against the glare of a late afternoon sun, he scoped the view of Lake Superior shimmering like a strip of blue tinsel on the horizon. He took a deep breath, wiped his hands on the bottom of his shirt and moved forward. The closer she got, the slower he walked. She was tall, lean and tan. She looked like one of those beach volleyball players he'd seen on cable. All he had to do was sound intelligent and not stare.

The woman carried herself with an air of professionalism that was at odds with the neglected property. She gave him a cheeky grin and extended her hand. "I'm Laura. Wanna buy it?"

He gave her a firm handshake. "Jack."

She quickly let go and slipped her hands into the back pockets of her denim shorts. Her cell phone hung from a holder clipped to her waist.

"Is it just the barn and not the house?" He kicked at a stone with the toe of his boot. "I'm in the process of relocating and the house I had rented was sold."

"Wow, that's a tough one."

"Yeah." He glanced at her.

She squinted, too, her hand shielding her eyes. "Sorry, but it's just the barn. There's an attached apartment, though. Take a look around."

"You wouldn't mind?" Jack had his reservations, but he might as well check it out. If nothing else, he'd met a pretty woman who'd brightened an otherwise frustrating day.

"If you don't mind me finishing the lawn. Go on in, the door's open."

"Perfect," he said.

Her expression changed as if it just dawned on her that she was alone in the sticks with a pretty good-sized stranger.

Jack gave her an encouraging nod. He might be tongue-tied, but he didn't pose a threat. Crossing the driveway, he stepped into the barn and flicked on a light switch to a single bare bulb hanging over a workshop area. A few old bales of hay lay stacked in a corner and dust covered everything.

Nosing around, he found a ladder leading to a lower level.

He climbed down and noticed cooler air mingled with the smell of stale oats. The walls looked solid and the foundation opened to an overgrown pasture by way of a sliding door.

He found the apartment and entered a big room containing two sets of bunk beds, a loft overlooking a small kitchenette, and a curtained entrance to a bathroom with a shower stall, sink and toilet.

He turned on the faucet. After a minor shudder, cloudy water spewed out, and then ran clear. Even the toilet flushed without trouble. He took the wrought-iron spiral staircase to the loft, testing each step. Sturdy. The loft was big enough for a twin bed and maybe a small dresser, but it would allow his daughter some privacy. She'd have to make do until they had a house of their own built.

Was moving Angie to the U.P. the right thing? His sister thought he was crazy. Angie would surely hate this compared to her frilly bedroom overlooking the river back home in Lansing, but it wouldn't be forever.

This felt right. And the timing was perfect. He rubbed his neck. Was this God's provision from out of a jam or just Jack's wishful thinking?

Looking out the back window of the apartment, he spotted a powder-blue sports car parked near the house. If that belonged to Laura, she had a decent job—probably in Houghton. If she lived here, why'd she let it go?

Outside, he caught the woman's attention and shouted, "Mind if I take a walk?"

She gave him a thumbs-up.

The property looked good as far as he could tell, but he'd have to see the survey. The gentle sloping field stretched to a small woods, then more open meadow. A slice of Lake Superior shimmered just beyond that.

He could picture his daughter here—riding horses, planting

a garden. An image of Angie picking the vegetables they could grow together was all it took. He came around the side of the barn and waited for Laura to notice him.

She drove the lawn mower toward him and shut it off. "What do you think?"

"I'm buying out a vet practice in town, but my goal is to work and live on the same property. I'm not sure if building a home first or the business is more appropriate."

"You're a vet?" Her eyebrows lifted, as if surprised. "This place would be perfect for you."

"I have a daughter, that's why I wanted to rent. Get to know the area better before committing."

"I'm not interested in renting. I need to sell."

Jack rubbed the stubble on his chin. "But should I buy a house or a practice facility? This place would work well as a vet's office."

Looking into her blue eyes for guidance he knew she couldn't give, he noticed her irises were rimmed in yellow. She had beautiful eyes that tilted up at the corners. His mouth formed the words before his mind registered. "What's your asking price? I'm interested in buying."

Chapter Two

Laura felt the weight of his stare and shifted her stance. This guy was big, well over six feet. He had an unruly mop of sandy blond hair with more than a day's growth of beard. He was rough-looking with a lumberjack quality that most women would admire. But Laura wasn't most women. He had a daughter. "How old is your daughter?"

He beamed like any proud parent, his blue eyes shining. "She's thirteen and she starts school after Labor Day."

"There's not much room in that apartment for a teenaged girl."

"We've had to adjust to tougher things."

What kind of things?

Laura's interest piqued. Any self-respecting girl would hate living in a barn.

He pointed toward Lake Superior. "Eventually, I could see myself building on the edge of those woods, as long as they're part of the twenty acres."

"Maybe I should call my Realtor." Laura grabbed her phone and dialed. When her Realtor finally answered, Laura explained the situation.

"I'll ask." Laura lowered her phone. "She wants to know if you've had dinner?"

He looked surprised. "No."

"He hasn't." Laura held his gaze. "Are you hungry? We can go through the papers over dinner if you have time. You can bring your daughter, too."

"I have the time, but Angie's not with me. She's at my sister's in Lansing."

"We'll meet you there." Laura disconnected and looked up. "I hope you like Italian."

"Some of my favorite food."

"The restaurant's in the center of town. You can't miss it. It's called Gino's."

"Mind if I follow you?" he asked.

"Not at all. I'll get my keys." Laura headed for the house. She turned in time to see Jack climb into his monster-sized SUV parked across the road. He was a big, tall man with a big truck.

She usually met with men in the safety of offices and restaurants to go over business plans, but this was different. Grabbing her purse, she locked the front door and walked to her car while Jack pulled into the drive. She caught him giving her the once-over, but then he quickly looked away.

She was used to men checking her out. Her looks were one of the challenges she'd faced at work—getting the tech heads to trust her and businessmen to take her seriously. Still, she couldn't help but wonder what Jack might look like if he shaved.

Slipping in behind the wheel, she turned the key but nothing happened. The car turned over but wouldn't start.

"Sounds like you're out of gas." He leaned close and smelled like sunshine and spice. His nearness gave her goose bumps.

"I guess I pushed it too far." She'd been back and forth to the hospital several times the last couple days. On her way home last night, the gas station in the four-corner town her mother lived near was closed.

"You can ride with me."

Laura looked up into those kind blue eyes of his, but she wasn't buying. "What did you say your last name was?"

He smiled, displaying perfectly even, white teeth—no doubt the handiwork of a good orthodontist. "Jack Stahl."

"Thanks, Dr. Stahl, but there's a gas can in the barn. I'll be just fine."

He backed away as she got out. "It's just Jack. I'll get the can if you show me where."

She hesitated only a moment before leading the way. She matched his long strides across the lawn and opened the barn door. "Where are you from?"

"East Lansing. What about you? You don't strike me as the U.P. type."

"What gives you that idea?"

He gestured toward her waist. "The latest in cell phones."

"What, no one in the U.P. has a cell phone?" She didn't want to admit that her mother lived alone, not yet.

"Yours is pretty high-tech. Are you a professor?"

She laughed. "No."

"Landscaper then, you mow a mean lawn." He actually winked before he picked up a five-gallon gas can as if it weighed nothing.

"Thanks." She focused on anything but him. Something about him made her feel off-kilter.

"Nice tractor." He pointed toward the old John Deere. "Antique?"

"It belonged to my father."

"Does it work?"

"I don't know." She followed him out.

Without a moment's hesitation, he reached in and popped her gas cover. She watched as he unscrewed the cap. His hands were large and broad with clean fingernails cut short. He wore a modest wedding ring, but he hadn't mentioned a wife. Was he divorced? It didn't matter. Like Anthony, he had a daughter.

"How far?"

His question scattered her thoughts. "What?"

"How far to the restaurant?"

"Five or six miles."

"I'll follow you, but you may want to stop and fill up just the same."

"Will do, Jack. I'll meet you there."

Jack took a deep breath before opening the door to the pizza parlor. "Italian, huh?"

"You can order pasta, pizza, even meatball subs." She gave him a quirky grin.

"I'll remember that." He held the door for her. When she passed by him, he inhaled her perfume. It was soft and incredibly pleasing. He hoped she didn't live next door. He was noticing things he'd be better off ignoring.

He spotted a middle-aged woman with a file laid open on the table. After the introductions had been made, Maddie Smith, the Realtor, smiled. "I hope you don't mind a booth," she whispered. "More private."

"Fine with me." Laura scooted in next to Maddie.

Jack sat across from them. Laura looked ready to get down to business. Surely that meant she was eager to part with the barn instead of negotiating. He didn't want to waste time haggling.

"What do you like on your pizza?" Maddie asked.

"Everything or nothing. I like it all. Whatever you choose is fine." Jack didn't care what they ate or drank. He wanted to put his offer on the table.

The waitress quickly took their order and left. Soon the restaurant started to fill up with customers.

Jack took a sip of his soft drink. "I need a place right away but I know the mortgage process doesn't work that fast."

He looked at Laura. Her brow furrowed slightly, so he touched her arm with reassurance. The softness of her skin registered, which reminded him to move his hand away. "Hear me out. I'm interested in making an offer."

She leaned back against the red vinyl of the booth.

He wasn't sure if he'd offended her with his touch or his honesty. Either way, he wasn't about to be discouraged. "I'd like to rent with the option to buy within a year at your listing price."

Laura sat forward. "You don't even know my listing price. How do you know you can afford it?"

"I can afford it."

Her eyes widened. "What if you decide after a month that there's too much work needed?"

"I can't see that happening, but if I pull out, I'll give you six more months rent so you can relist."

She shook her head. "I have to sell. Can you tell me what's stopping you from buying?"

Jack also leaned forward. "I have a daughter to consider. I think this place might be good for us. But if I'm wrong, I need the ability to change gears."

"I see."

Maddie, who quietly watched their exchange, cleared her throat. "We can look at a land contract. It's a little more than just renting yet not quite buying it outright." They both glanced her way as she explained the specifics.

Maddie wanted him to have it. Of course she did, she was the Realtor, but Jack couldn't help but feel like Maddie was in his corner. She'd just offered a plan that fell somewhere in the middle of what they both wanted.

Laura looked skeptical but in control. "What if he defaults?"

"Pardon me for sounding arrogant, but money's not an issue. In fact, if you decide to sell the house, I'd be interested in that, too, but I won't be taken for a sap."

"You'd have the deed, dear." Maddie turned to Laura as if he'd never spoken. "You'd simply be back where you are now, looking for a new buyer, only you'd keep the agreed down payment for your trouble."

Laura looked him straight in the eye, judging him, weighing his words. "You said you could buy the house, too? Pardon me for being nosy, but I didn't think vets made that much."

She'd just put him in his place. Whatever she did for a living, the sleek image of a shark came to mind. He shifted under her direct gaze. "I sold off my part of a limited partnership for a generous sum. I have other investments as well. The point is that my daughter needs new surroundings and so do I. I could retire, but being a vet is no less a calling than any other type of doctor. I'm buying out a nearby practice so the guy can retire. This area is perfect for many reasons. Check my credit, my bank accounts, whatever it takes to prove my credibility."

That earned him a look of surprise from Laura. He'd managed to impress her and for some odd reason, that pleased him.

After a brief silence, she smiled deliberately. "Forgive me, Dr. Stahl, but I tend to look for all the pitfalls. This is my mother's house and barn. I'm acting in her best interest, but I think we can move forward."

"Of course we can," Maddie said with a wave of her hand as if it all were nothing. "I'll have the papers drawn up in the morning, then meet with you both again, say tomorrow at noon at the house? Dr. Stahl, I need you to sign a credit release." Maddie searched her file, until she produced the document and laid it upon the table.

He had nothing to hide. He took the offered pen, signed his name and dated it. "And, please, it's just Jack."

They discussed the details, and even after acting like he could buy the world, Laura didn't attempt to pinch him for more. The down payment was modest.

"So that's it." Laura set down the pen.

"I'm buying your barn and twenty." A slow grin spread

across his face and then he remembered. "I have movers scheduled for this weekend."

Laura bit her bottom lip. "I have to clear out the barn, but that shouldn't be a problem."

"If you'd like, I can buy what's in there for another two thousand." He wanted that tractor.

Laura shook her head. "I need to sort through things first. There might not be anything of worth."

Again, she didn't take advantage of the situation. She might be deadly direct in negotiations, but she had integrity. "Do you mind if I swing by early tomorrow and start cleaning?"

"Does that work for you, Laura?" Maddie asked.

"It does."

Jack looked at the last name on the listing agreement. "So tell me, what nationality is *Tee-ovo?*"

Laura tipped her head and laughed softly. Her pretty eyes slanted even more. "You're saying it wrong. It's pronounced *Toy-vo.* It was my great-grandfather's first name but it got turned around during immigration. I'm Finnish on both sides."

"Pretty name." *For a pretty woman.* He shouldn't like the color that stole over her cheeks, knowing he'd put it there with such a simple compliment, but he did.

He watched Laura's attention waver by the arrival of the pizza. She reached for a piece.

"Does anyone mind if I say grace?" He might as well let her know he was a man of faith right up front.

Laura's eyes narrowed as if judging him, questioning his sincerity. She shrugged her shoulders. "Go ahead."

"Wonderful." Maddie laid a slice on her plate.

Jack offered up his simple thanks and asked a special blessing upon both Maddie and Laura. Then a cell phone rang.

"I'm sorry." Laura got up from the table and headed outside.

"She's in sales," Maddie said with an indulgent smile.

Jack nodded, thinking that made perfect sense.

* * *

Laura closed her phone. Mr. Albertson wanted to wait for her return before signing. Her sales manager, Jeff, offered to step in and close the deal, but Mr. Albertson wouldn't hear of it. He didn't trust Albertson Manufacturing's I.T. support to anyone but Laura.

It felt good to be that respected by a client. Laura hadn't impressed anyone in her family with her climb up the corporate ladder from computer programming geek to one of their top salespeople.

She'd managed to impress Jack Stahl, though. He'd given her a look of admiration over the negotiation table. Jack seemed like the kind of man who was used to getting his own way, but she hadn't let that sway her. Hearing him pray had been surprising. When he asked a special blessing over her and Maddie, softness had crept into her heart.

Laura had stopped looking to God for help when she was a kid, but she wouldn't mind a little divine assistance now. With her manager pressing for a return date she couldn't give, and her mother's blood pressure still unstable, Laura hoped things got back to normal fast. Until then, she'd work as much as she could from here. She had her laptop, but the sooner she got back to work, the better.

Chapter Three

The next morning Jack called his sister from his motel room to let her know that he'd be home later than planned. He asked if she'd keep Angie one more night. His daughter was still asleep, so there wasn't a chance to talk to her. He'd soften the blow of their new home in person.

After a quick breakfast at a local diner, Jack stopped at the school office to confirm Angie's enrollment, then he turned down the road toward Laura's. After pulling in the drive and shutting off the motor, he checked his watch. Eight-thirty. The Realtor wasn't coming until noon so he had plenty of time. He stared at his barn, soon to be home, and his hands itched to grab his tools and start renovating. But cleaning was the first priority.

He glanced at the house. Was Laura an early riser? His wife used to sleep in on Saturdays. Jack had never succeeded in getting Joanne up early in the morning to kayak with him on the river near their town house. No matter how hard he pushed or pleaded, she hated mornings and the water. If only Jack had paid more attention to her fears.

He got out of his truck, shifting a box of cleaning supplies on his hip. Taking care not to dump the contents that rattled and clanged, he walked to the side door of the barn and turned the knob. Locked. Laura had the key.

He headed toward the porch and rapped on the kitchen door. Laura's sleek blue convertible sat in the driveway. That car didn't belong in this part of the U.P. where the winters were long and harsh. He knocked again.

The curtains parted abruptly and Laura peeked through, her cell phone against her ear. She gestured for him to hold on. He waited only a few moments until she opened the door. "You're here early."

He took in the picture she presented, starting at her bare feet with toenails painted bright purple. She wore khaki shorts and a matching T-shirt.

He cleared his throat. "I'm sorry. The door to the barn is locked. Can I have the key?"

She scanned his box of cleaning supplies. "Wouldn't it be easier to hire someone?"

"Maybe, but I need to get to know my place hands-on," he said.

"Give me a minute and I'll join you. I need to go through my dad's stuff anyway."

Jack shifted his box. He didn't want her invading his space, distracting him. "It's dirty out there. I can handle it."

"What, I can't get dirty?" She reached for a key tied to a faded blue ribbon and handed it to him. "Besides, I can show you some of my dad's tools in case you want to buy them. I'll meet you there in a few minutes."

Jack stood staring at the doorknob, key in hand. It'd been a long time since he'd noticed another woman with interest. And it was impossible not to notice Laura Toivo. Losing Joanne had left a gaping hole in his world, but he was finally putting his life back together. And that meant focusing on his kids. Building a secure environment for Angie. He didn't have the time or energy to date.

He refused to find a high-strung saleswoman like Laura desirable. She had *career first family second* written all over her. Definitely not what he wanted. If only he didn't find tall, blue-eyed blondes attractive.

Laura pulled on her sneakers from under the kitchen table, where she'd kicked them off last night. Just that small movement caused sweat to bead along her brow. Morning and already it was a scorcher. Unusual for late August in the U.P.

She opened her mother's cupboard and grabbed an old-fashioned pitcher. She smiled when she thought of the look Jack had given her on the porch. She should be used to it by now—the eager eyes most men wore when they noticed her. But Jack's expression had been softer, sweeter somehow. He had turned beet red. He was too cute. Something she certainly had no business noticing.

She quickly made lemonade, grabbed a couple of ice-filled glasses, and headed out the door. It was as good a time as any to go through her dad's things. And she might as well get to know Jack, now that he was going to be living across the driveway from her mother.

As Jack scrubbed the toilet, he heard Laura's approach with a clinking of glass. He looked up.

"Want some lemonade?" She stood in the doorway brandishing a metal tray topped with refreshments like some sort of shield.

"Sure."

"Ugh, that's just gross." She placed an icy glass on the edge of the sink. "I'm sorry this place is in such sad shape. It's too much for my mother to keep up, so we decided to sell it."

"It's not so bad." Jack took a long drink. It made sense, the neglected property, the outdated wiring. He'd bet Laura didn't live anywhere near here. Good thing, too. Out of sight, out of mind. He went back to the toilet with a vengeance. "Is it just you and your mom?"

"Just the two of us."

"No brothers or sisters in the area?"

"Nope." After setting down her tray, she moved toward a dusty radio perched on an even dustier shelf. "Do you mind?"

"Go ahead."

She turned the knob with sounds of static blips until she settled on a station. "Do you like jazz?"

"Not really. But it's coming in clearly." Jack stood and stretched his back. He fumbled through his box for a can of foaming bathroom cleaner. He sprayed the sink and the tiled walls.

"Let me guess, you like country." She'd parked herself on a nearby stool, sweating glass of lemonade in hand.

"What's wrong with country?" He'd grown to love country music since it was often played in the horse barns where he'd made house calls.

Her expression clearly showed that he'd dropped a tick or two on her impressed scale. "Nothing. It's just so typical up here."

Why'd he care what she thought? "My parents used to summer near here when I was a kid."

"Is that what made you choose this area?"

"That and the chance to buy out Dr. Walter's practice." He emptied his glass with a rattle of ice. "My daughter and I need a change in scenery and my son's college is nearby. The location seemed perfect."

"You know, you're sticking her in the middle of nowhere. Thirteen's a tough age."

What could *she* possibly know about it? "Do you have kids?"

Her expression took on a strained, almost haunted look. "No. I've never been married, but I got close once."

"What happened?" He shouldn't have asked, but the words slipped out. He could have kicked himself for caring about the answer. He didn't want to care about what Laura might have been through. He didn't want to care. Period.

She shrugged. "He had a young daughter who didn't want me for a stepmother."

Jack could tell the admission hurt. He wondered why she hadn't gotten along with this guy's kid. Probably too busy with her job. Kids knew that stuff. They picked up on priorities.

"What about you?"

Jack hesitated. "Widowed."

Her expression changed to pity. "Oh, I'm so sorry."

He let out a sigh. "It's been two years this past June."

She sipped her lemonade, looking more composed. "That must be hard on your kids."

You have no idea.

He wiped down the wall with a rag, keeping busy, but he suddenly found himself wanting to unload, and Laura was surprisingly easy to talk to. It wasn't as if she'd stick around, so what harm was it to confess a few insecurities? "Sometimes, I feel like a blind man searching for a book in the braille section of a library. Only, I don't know the title."

"I'm sure you'll find it, just like you found this property when you needed it most."

She couldn't possibly know how God had answered his prayer. He needed to trust God to lead him to the book—to lead him through this. Good things took time and commitment. He had plenty of both to make this place a real home. A place where Angie could grow out of her grief. A place where he could release his regrets. "Thanks."

"I hope this property proves to be a blessing for you and your daughter, like it was for my dad. I think he'd approve of your plans if he were here."

Jack stopped cleaning and turned to look at her. She didn't strike him as having a rock-solid faith, but then he didn't know what was in Laura's heart when it came to God. "I take it your father's dead."

"When I was your daughter's age my dad died at work from a chemical leak." Her voice lowered.

"I'm sorry."

She shrugged. "The worst part was never saying goodbye, you know?"

Jack looked away. "Yeah, I know."

After a few moments of silence, she popped off the stool and changed the subject. "Want more to drink?"

"No, but thank you."

"Before I sort through the stuff in the barn, was there anything that caught your eye?"

What a loaded question. He followed her, though, noticing her height. He was pushing six-four and the top of her head would graze his nose if they stood close. But he didn't want to consider standing close to Laura.

"I'd love to buy that old tractor and the lawn mower. How much do you want for them?"

"How much are you willing to pay?" she asked.

He'd already offered her two thousand for the lot, but he'd play her game. It was more fun than cleaning. "What kind of sales do you do?"

"Business solutions."

"No wonder," he said with a smile.

"What?"

"Answer a question with a question, is that your motto?"

She gave him a cheeky grin. "The client should always give me the number and I'll work it from there."

Jack put his hands in the pockets of his worn jeans. He liked her. She was edgy, maybe even a little cocky, but he liked her. "Well, Ms. Toivo, name your price and I'll count it as fair."

"Just Laura. And if you show me what tools are worth keeping, then the tractor is yours for eight hundred. I have to keep the lawnmower until I find a reasonable landscaper."

"You give me the mower, and I'll make sure your mother's lawn is kept neat as a pin."

She smiled and extended her hand. "You've got yourself a deal. And you're good. You never gave anything away. Shall we shake on it?"

He grasped her hand firmly and then noticed a dusty spider's web clinging to her head. "Seems you've got a cobweb in your hair."

He felt her hand tremble and her eyes widened in fear. "Get it off, please, get it off."

Without letting go, he stepped closer. He swiped his fingers through her silky hair, taking the sticky fibers with him. He wiped his hand on the back of his jeans. "It's gone."

She pulled back and frantically turned around. "Are there any more? Please don't tell me if anything is crawling anywhere, just brush it off."

"Nothing. You're fine."

She faced him, her cheeks pink. "Thanks."

The space between them suddenly shrunk, so Jack backed up.

Laura must have felt it too, because she shifted from one foot to the other looking confused. "So, your movers are coming this weekend?"

Jack cleared his throat. "We should be here by late afternoon or early evening on Saturday. Like I said last night, I want to get my daughter settled before school starts. Are you sure that won't cause a problem?"

"Not at all." She threw her arms wide. "I'll get this stuff out of here as soon as possible and the place is yours."

"Perfect. Now, how about a look at those tools."

Jack didn't need another complication in his life, especially an attractive neighbor. He needed to concentrate on Angie. He wanted to prove that he could be the kind of father his daughter needed. Involved and attentive, not distracted by a beautiful blonde.

* * *

Later that day, Laura straightened her shoulders and entered her mother's hospital room. The nurses had her mom sitting in a chair looking nearly normal except for the droop on the left side of her face. A bouquet of balloons rested in the far corner— no doubt from cousin Nancy and her kids. She noticed a small arrangement perched on the bedside table. "Where'd you get the flowers?"

"Maddie Smith, from the real estate office."

Laura's heart sank. She'd struggled with how to break the news to her mother that she'd sold the property. Even though her mom had agreed to list the barn, Laura knew her mother would blame her for having to sell it. Seemed like ever since Laura was a kid, she couldn't do anything right in her mother's eyes.

Laura had been a daddy's girl. She'd felt like her birth had come between her parents. That her mother had resented her for creating some rift between them. She remembered overhearing her mom tell her dad that he was spoiling his daughter rotten.

"Any bites? I guess it's early yet." Her mother's speech had also improved.

"A guy stopped by yesterday." She just couldn't fess up to the land contract.

Her mother's eye closed and then she shrugged her good shoulder. "Well, it's a nice piece of property, don't go giving it away."

"I won't." Jack had paid the listing price without flinching. Surely, that would please her mother, but it wouldn't hurt to give her mom a little more time to get used to the idea of selling.

"Have you seen your cousin Nancy?"

"No."

"You should see her children. Her youngest is a cute little thing."

"Uh-huh." Since when did her mother like kids? Growing

up, Laura wasn't allowed too many friends over because her mother didn't like the noise or the mess. Her mother didn't like all that commotion. Laura had spent her share of time at Nancy's because of that.

A quick knock on the door and Aunt Nelda peeked in. "I hope you're in the mood for company."

Her aunt's three grandchildren scampered across the room. They surrounded Laura's mom, wide-eyed with wonder, asking questions about her mother's drooping face all at once, failing to use their inside voices. But her mother clearly enjoyed the attention, and that surprised Laura.

"Maddie called me," Aunt Nelda said with a nod toward the hall.

Laura took the hint. "Mom? Aunt Nelda and I are going to get ginger ale for everyone. Will you be okay?"

Her mom shooed them away and returned to her tale about her hospital stay. The kids wore rapt expressions, and Laura's heart twisted. Her mom had never entertained *her* with stories when she was kid. Not even a bedtime story. That had been left for her dad to do. And then he'd died.

"The kids love her," Aunt Nelda whispered.

Laura stared at her mom a moment longer. Who'd have guessed? She followed her aunt out. "Did Maddie tell you we found a buyer?"

Her aunt grinned. "A handsome doctor from Lansing, who just happens to be single."

Laura shook her head. "He's a veterinarian, a widower, with two kids, one's a thirteen-year-old girl. I doubt he's interested."

"He's a man. They're always interested." Her aunt's smile was positively devious.

"I'm not interested." Since her broken engagement to Anthony, Laura had vowed she'd never be anyone's stepmother.

"Maybe I'm thinking of Nancy," her aunt teased.

Laura rolled her eyes. The thought of Jack Stahl dating her

cousin made her teeth clench, which was ridiculous. Like she'd told her aunt, *she* wasn't the least bit interested.

"Did you tell your mother?" Aunt Nelda asked.

"Not yet."

Aunt Nelda nodded with understanding. "See, we made the right choice. Everything happened just like it was supposed to."

Laura had grown up going to a church that spoke of miracles. They never seemed to happen for her, though. Maybe they didn't exist. She worked hard, and made choices. But it was one big, fat coincidence when Dr. Jack Stahl happened to be driving by yesterday. "Let's hope Mom agrees with you."

Aunt Nelda frowned. "When are you going to tell her?"

"When the time is right." Laura wished God would perform a miracle with her mother. She could use the help.

Chapter Four

That Saturday evening, Laura returned from the hospital to find a moving truck parked in the drive. Two men and Jack unloaded boxes and plastic-wrapped furniture into the clean and empty barn. A tall, lanky girl with one long, dark braid sat on the porch swing looking lost.

Laura parked her car and put up the top just in case it rained. The weather had been hot and humid. She eyed the girl on the porch who watched the movers with annoyance. Poor kid.

"You must be Jack's daughter." Keeping her distance, Laura sat on the top step of the porch. "My name is Laura."

"Mine's Angie," the girl said softly.

Sensing the kid's reluctance to chat, Laura didn't want to push. She rose to leave, but the stark grief pooled in the girl's blue eyes stopped her cold.

"Moving is tough," Laura quickly said. "My mom's lived here for thirty-three years. She's in the hospital right now and hates it. I tried to get her to move into an old folk's home but she said she'd rather live in a barn. I can't blame her a bit. Barns probably smell better."

She spotted Jack coming toward them. She cringed when she realized the kid had reduced her to rambling. Besides,

Laura's heart went out to her. "Have you seen the inside of the apartment yet?"

Angie nodded and rolled her eyes.

Ouch.

Jack stepped onto the porch, his color high. "Laura, this is my daughter, Angie."

"We've met. If you're interested, I'd be happy to fix you dinner, but I'm no gourmet cook. Either of you like macaroni salad and sandwiches?" Laura didn't know where that offer had come from, but it seemed like the neighborly thing to do.

Angie shrugged her shoulders. She looked like she wanted to disappear.

"Come on, Ange, what do you say to Ms. Toivo?" Jack said.

A teenager living in a barn, even with a cute little apartment, was not a good idea. Angie probably thought her father had taken leave of whatever sense he might possess by moving up here.

"Please, no need to call me that. Makes me sound like an old lady." She looked at Angie, hoping Jack didn't mind that she'd just counteracted his instructions. "Just Laura, okay?"

"Okay." Angie glanced back at her dad.

Jack didn't look confident about what to do with her, but his eyes narrowed in some form of communication.

His daughter evidently understood. With a sigh, she rose from the bench swing. "Point me to your pots and pans. I can help."

Laura unlocked the door to the kitchen. "Good, because I need all the help I can get."

"Ange, you go on ahead with Laura. I'll finish unloading. We don't have much more," Jack said.

Angie nodded, but her shoulders drooped.

Laura had heard that junior high girls might as well be aliens. One of the tech guys at work constantly complained about his daughter's changing attitudes—nice one minute, grouchy the next. She couldn't blame Angie. Who'd want to move here anyway?

"Your dad said you lived in East Lansing—anywhere near Michigan State? That's a pretty college campus."

No answer, just a shrug of skinny shoulders as they went inside.

"Living in the country will grow on you, kind of like mold." Laura released a nervous laugh.

No response, not even a hint of a smile.

Great. Laura set her purse on the kitchen table. "So—" She clapped her hands together. "Are you good with a knife?"

Angie looked surprised. "I guess."

Laura opened the refrigerator. "Let's see, carrots, cukes, pickles, celery and hard-boiled eggs. You can cut these up into a big bowl. I'll start the pasta and sandwiches."

"Where's your big bowls?"

Laura looked through her mother's cupboards and found some. "How's this?"

"Fine."

Laura kept busy. She gathered the fixings for turkey sandwiches and then grabbed a pot, causing all the other pans to rattle and spill out of the cupboard. She glanced at Angie. A ghost of a smile hovered at the corners of the girl's lips.

"Do you live here?" Angie's quiet voice asked.

"No. This is my mother's house."

"What's the matter with her—your mom?"

Laura heard the slight tremor in Angie's voice. It still hurt. Of course it did. Laura still felt twinges when she thought of her dad. She filled the pot with water and set it on the burner. "She had a stroke. Her blood pressure's too high for her to come home yet."

"Oh."

Laura dumped macaroni into the pot and turned on the gas. She knew Angie watched her every move as she slathered a piece of bread. "Do you like mayo? I didn't think to ask."

"It doesn't matter."

"What do you like to drink? I've got milk, Diet Coke and prune juice." Laura looked at Angie, hoping for a smile.

Nothing. And then finally, "Milk's fine."

Laura set the table when a hissing sound caught her attention. She turned in time to see bubbling water foam over the rim of the pot and onto the stove. The gas burner flared red. Laura ran to grab the pot, and gasped when she burned her fingers.

Angie actually laughed. "You put the pasta in too soon. You've got to wait until the water boils."

Laura finally relaxed. "Why didn't you tell me? I make macaroni like, never."

Angie laughed again. "I used to make macaroni and cheese from the box all the time, but now we get the microwave kind."

"I didn't know there was a microwave kind." Laura's meals were either eaten out, ordered in or frozen entrees.

"Don't you cook?" Angie asked.

"I do breakfast. Eggs and toast."

Angie shook her head then took over. She fished in a drawer for potholders, grabbed the hot pot and dumped the contents into the colander.

"Hey, you know what you're doing," Laura said.

Angie ran the noodles under cold water. "I help with dinner at home."

Laura stepped closer and peeked into the sink. "Are they done?"

"They're okay."

Laura fished a limp noodle from the colander and popped it in her mouth. "I guess they'll have to do."

"It'll taste better once I mix in the veggies, eggs and mayo."

"Obviously, you've done this before," Laura said.

Angie gave her a "the artist isn't finished" look. "Salt and pepper?"

"Whoa." Laura jumped when the screen door suddenly slammed shut with a gust of wind. She didn't realize it had been left open.

Then Angie screeched.

"What's the matter?" Laura's heart jumped into her throat. "What *is* that?"

Laura saw a small black form dart through the kitchen. "It's just a bat."

"Eeeeew, gross," Angie breathed.

"He won't hurt you," Laura said.

"I must have left the screen open," Angie whined. "Can you get it out?"

Laura took control by fetching a plastic bowl. She'd chased bats out of her mother's house ever since she was a kid. It was no big deal. She placed her finger on her lips and crept into the living room.

"But I thought bats were deaf," Angie whispered.

"No, they're blind. They use radar or something to fly." Laura quietly closed the door to the upstairs, then the door to the laundry room and spare room. And then waited for the bat to land.

Angie ducked under a magazine she grabbed from the coffee table when the black ball of fur zoomed through the air. But she stayed quiet.

The minutes ticked by until finally the bat gripped a torn piece of wallpaper in the dining room.

Angie's eyes went wide as plates, when Laura lifted the large bowl overhead. "What are you going to do?"

"You'll see." Laura tiptoed toward the bat.

Angie scooted behind Laura, not wanting to be left alone in the open.

"Don't move," Laura breathed.

Angie folded herself into Laura's back. "I won't."

Laura cupped the bowl against the wall, trapping the bat underneath. It flapped then settled down. "Get me that macaroni box. Open it flat so I can slip it between the wall and the bowl."

Angie looked unsure, but she ran to the kitchen and returned with a flattened box.

Laura kept one hand on the bowl and wedged the cardboard underneath the rim.

"You did it," Angie said with a trace of awe.

"Yup." Laura headed for the porch. She set the bowl down and lifted the cardboard lid, then stepped back. The bat flew out against a darkening, angry-looking sky.

"Is it gone?" Angie whispered from the other side of the screen door.

"Yes."

"I thought bats only came out at night."

"Usually just before dark, to get the bugs. I think they're cute."

"You're crazy. They make nests in your hair and stink."

Laura laughed. "Who told you that?"

Angie shrugged. "I dunno. Isn't it true?"

"Nope, not true. You'll get used to them."

Angie didn't look like she believed Laura, but she sighed. "I've got a lot of stuff to get used to."

Jack wiped his hands on his shirt. "Are you guys sure you won't stay for a bite to eat?" He overstepped Laura's invitation by offering food to the movers, but it had taken longer than he thought to finish up and he was starving.

"Thanks, but we've got to get back," one of the movers said.

Jack nodded, relieved. He gave each man a tip and shook their hands before they climbed into the moving truck. A low rumble of thunder in the distance made Jack thank God for keeping the rain away until the last of his boxes were unloaded and stacked in the barn. Now, it could rain buckets for all he cared.

A fork of pink lightning skittered across the sky and the wind picked up as he stepped onto the porch and stopped. Through the screen door, he caught a scene in the kitchen that made his jaw drop. Angie stirred something in a big bowl and Laura placed a tray of sandwiches on the table.

Jack checked his watch. It had been over an hour and a half

but the girls didn't seem to have noticed his delay. They chatted comfortably and Jack thought he heard a few giggles. He wiped the sweat from his brow and noticed a plastic bowl at his feet beside a piece of cardboard. He picked them up and knocked on the door.

"Come in, Jack," Laura said.

He handed her the bowl. "Something smells good."

"Eeewww, Dad, you better wash your hands. There was a bat in there. You'll get rabies."

Jack grinned. "You can't get rabies from a bowl. What was in here, a bat? Who caught it?"

Laura squared her shoulders, looking pleased. "I did. With your daughter's help, of course. Welcome to the Upper Peninsula of Michigan."

Jack raised his eyebrows.

"Angie has also saved the macaroni salad from becoming a pile of mush."

"How'd she do that?"

"Laura doesn't know how to cook pasta." Angie looked more amused than disgusted.

And Laura ignored the comment as if she'd known his daughter longer than just a couple hours. "We have turkey sandwiches, too."

"Sounds great." Jack looked around quickly. "I better wash up."

Laura guided his way. "Down the hallway off the dining room. The door to your right, it's closed but no one's in there."

Then Angie giggled. "Use lots of soap, so you get the bat stink off."

Laura joined in with a soft laugh.

Jack nodded. It wasn't that funny, but he clamped his lips shut and entered the bathroom. He didn't want to ruin a private joke by making someone explain it. Besides, he was tired of trying so hard with Angie. He was just plain tired.

As he dried his hands, he thought about what Angie had said about Laura. How could someone not know how to make macaroni? The instructions were right there, easy as can be. He returned to the kitchen and took a seat at the retro metal-legged table with matching red, vinyl-covered chairs.

"Water, Diet Coke or prune juice?" Laura asked.

His daughter giggled again.

After all the arguing they'd done about the move, he'd nearly forgotten how much he loved the sound. After driving nine hours with Angie, he'd rather examine a porcupine. Now she laughed as if nothing had ever been wrong. He'd never figure her out. "Water's fine. I can get it."

"Sit, sit." Laura gestured with her hands.

He sat across from Angie and they waited for Laura. Then Jack bowed his head.

"Oh," Laura whispered.

Jack peeked up at her. "Do you mind?" He caught her quick glance at Angie, who rolled her eyes.

"Not at all." She bowed her head and waited.

Jack took a deep breath. "Dear Lord, thank You for this wonderful food and bless those who prepared it. Oh, and please protect me from rabies and any bat stink I might have missed. Amen." He reached for a napkin and a rumble of thunder echoed through the air.

"I think He heard you." Laura scooped pasta onto her plate, and then looked at him. "I didn't think you could make fun when you prayed."

"God made us with a sense of humor, why wouldn't He have one, too?"

Laura cocked her head. Her chin-length blond hair had been pushed back with a headband. It made her look young and vulnerable. "I never thought of it like that."

He quickly looked away as he took the bowl of macaroni salad from her.

"I love thunderstorms," Angie said, digging into the pile of sandwiches.

"Ugh, why?" Laura said.

"I dunno." His daughter tossed her head and flipped the braid off her shoulder. "I just do."

Laura took a bite of the macaroni salad. "Wow, this is really good."

"Thanks. But I think it still needs something."

Jack watched in amazement at the easiness between them. His daughter didn't warm up to strangers. Lately, she didn't warm up to anyone. "So, how'd the bat get in the house?"

"I left the screen door open," Angie said.

Laura looked at him. "It was an accident. I think the bat was looking for a place to ride out the storm. We're supposed to get a real soaker. We need the rain."

Just then a flicker of lightning brightened the room and a crash of thunder shook the house. The fluorescent light overhead dimmed, flickered and then went out.

"There goes the power," Laura whispered. "I hate it when this happens."

Her admission surprised him. The bat in the house didn't rattle her, neither did his daughter. Other than spider webs, Jack didn't think Laura Toivo scared easily. Yet the sounds of a storm building outside made her anxious. "How long does it stay out?"

"Who knows?" Laura got up from the table, leaving her sandwich half-eaten. She rummaged through one of the kitchen drawers and pulled out some taper candles. Sticking a few into skinny juice glasses, she lit them and placed a couple on the table. "We've got plenty of candles if you'd like some to take to the apartment."

"That'd be great."

"Yeah, *great*," Angie muttered.

"It's only for a while, Ange." Jack squeezed his daughter's hand.

She pulled away. "Where am I going to put my clothes?"

Another flash of lightning followed by a deafening crack of

thunder and Laura jumped. She focused on her plate, looking uncertain, almost shy. "It's late and probably too dark to get unloaded in the apartment tonight. There's plenty of room if you'd like to stay here tonight."

Jack stared at her. They were practically strangers. "We couldn't put you to all the trouble."

"Really, it's no problem." But she sounded nervous.

Another crack of thunder boomed while lightning danced through the windows. The wind whipped and, with a roar, a deluge of rain fell followed by heavier beats. He heard the clicking of ice balls ricocheting off the side porch.

Angie ran to the screen door, water spraying in from outside. "Dad, we can't go out there. It's hailing."

"Close the door, Ange." He glanced back at Laura who twisted her napkin. She looked tense.

"To be honest, with a storm like this, I wouldn't mind the company."

He knew Laura's invitation had more to do with her fear of storms than anything else. Cocky, capable businesswoman, Laura Toivo was scared of a thunderstorm. An unexpected urge to protect her assaulted him. But staying overnight under the same roof couldn't be a good idea. He'd prefer to keep his attractive neighbor at a safe distance across the lawn and driveway.

Angie noticed his hesitation. "Come on, Dad. How are we going to find anything in the dark? Let's just stay here with Laura."

"Okay, okay. We'll stay. Now, could someone pass me another sandwich?" But something more than hunger twisted his gut. His magnetic spark of interest flashed into full-blown attraction.

Chapter Five

"**Y**our room is this way." Laura gathered sheets from the linen closet. Angie followed her down the hall cupping a flickering candle.

She opened the door to her old bedroom just as lightning streaked across the sky, brightening the room. The downpour had settled into soft rain, but the storm still lingered.

"It's huge," Angie said. "This was yours?"

"All mine." Laura walked to the bed and pulled off the frilly coverlet. "Being an only child has its perks."

Angie set the candle down and helped her strip the bed.

"My bedroom's tiny."

"Small can be cozy." Laura shook out the sheets. She remade the four-poster canopy bed with Angie's help, aligning the old white-ruffled spread back into place.

Laura sighed. Potential lay everywhere in this house, but her mother refused to see it. The windows overlooked the backyard, complete with a view of Lake Superior. Laura had done a ton of dreaming staring out those windows.

"The bathroom is next door." Laura placed a couple towels and a washcloth on the desk then scooped up the discarded sheets.

"Where's my dad sleeping?" Angie asked.

"A spare bedroom next to this one."

"Great, I'm beat," said a masculine voice.

Laura's heart skittered to a halt along with her footsteps. Jack filled the doorway. The front of his T-shirt showed wet spots from washing their dinner dishes. She tried not to stare. "I'll get more clean sheets." She hurried out into the hall, turning to peek back in. "Good night, Angie."

"Night, Laura." Angie smiled.

Laura dashed for the closet. Stuffing the old bedding into a hamper, she grabbed fresh linens for Jack. Her breath came quick as if she'd run up a flight of stairs.

She entered the spare room and lit an oil lantern. She could hear the muffled voices of Jack and Angie through the wall. Even if Jack made her feel a little unsettled, it was definitely a comfort having them here. She'd sleep better knowing someone else was in the house.

Laura pulled off the quilt and sheets of the twin bed, re-membering how Angie had perked up when Jack had called her brother, Ben, to check on him after the storm had settled.

Laura had always wanted a brother or sister—someone to talk to or even fight with, anything to cut through the silence of growing up.

"Thanks again. You didn't have to do this." Jack's voice was low, but unsure. Self-conscious.

"But I think Angie's glad. Sort of a transition before the 'barn.'" Laura made quote marks with her fingers.

He laughed softly. "You're probably right. Can I help with that?"

She felt him lean toward her and her pulse picked up speed. "No problem, I got it."

She tucked the top sheet under the corner of the mattress then reached for the quilt. He bent to grab it, too. They were close. They both straightened. A low rumble of thunder shook the ground, and Laura dropped the quilt.

"You sure you're okay?" The corners of Jack's mouth twitched.

"I just don't like storms. They make me nervous."

"I thought salespeople were fearless." Jack picked up the quilt.

"We're a neurotic bunch, but we act like we've got it all together."

Jack laughed, a deep, rich sound.

"What about you? Isn't there anything you're afraid of?" she asked.

Jack spread the quilt over the bed then sat on the edge. "Thirteen-year-old girls and eighteen-year-old boys out on their own for the first time."

Laura looked into his troubled eyes. He worried about his kids. She imagined all parents did that—some more than others. But Jack admitted his concerns. He didn't act like he had all the answers and that made him that much more appealing. "Why not stay in Lansing? Wouldn't that have been easier?"

He looked away and fluffed the pillow. "Angie started hanging out with the wrong kids, skipping class and giving my sister a hard time about where she was headed after school. I caught her smoking cigarettes in our backyard. That's not my Angie. We needed a change, starting with me. I need to be around more, plain and simple."

Lightning flashed and thunder grumbled in the distance. Laura wiped her hands along the sides of her shorts. "Sounds like you're doing the right thing, then."

Jack ran a hand through his hair. "I hope so."

She didn't know what it was like to be a parent, but she knew what it was like to be a kid. Jack struck her as a dad who cared, deeply. Angie had a parent who tried. That had to count for something.

"It's late," Laura said. "I'll see you in the morning."

"Good night, and thanks." His hair stuck up in odd directions and his eyelids were puffy.

The urge to smooth back his hair tugged at Laura. The worst part was that he looked like he might welcome her touch.

"Good night, Jack." She hurried out the door before she gave in to her impulse.

Laura breathed in the scent of fresh-brewed coffee and sizzling bacon as she bustled around the kitchen hoping the aroma of food teased the senses of her guests enough to wake them. It was nearly nine o'clock and she had to head out to the hospital. After her pasta fiasco, she wanted to prove to Angie that she could make breakfast.

She poured herself a cup of coffee and listened. She heard male humming coming from outside. She didn't recognize the tune but the sweet sound intrigued her.

With a light knock, Jack opened the screen door and stepped into the kitchen. "Morning."

"You're up."

"Just getting a head start on unpacking. Is that coffee up for grabs?"

"Sure is. I'll have breakfast ready in a minute if you're interested."

Jack grabbed a mug from the counter and filled it with coffee, milk and sugar—just like Laura took hers. "I'm starved."

She smiled. "What were you humming?"

His cheeks flushed. "Just an old hymn."

Laura smiled. It had been ages since she heard a male voice in this house, especially in the morning. "My dad used to sing."

Jack nodded. "Sounds like you were pretty close to him."

"I was."

He sipped his coffee. "This is good."

Laura wrinkled her nose. "My mom's grocery-store variety. Too bad I didn't bring the good stuff. There's this awesome coffee shop around the corner from my condo. They roast their own beans."

He laughed. "So you like more cultured coffee?"

She turned the slices of bacon over. "Don't you?"

"I don't care as long as it's hot and fresh. Just don't give me decaf."

"You'll fit right in up here. You can't get good coffee without driving into Houghton or Hancock."

"This area is not without culture."

The colleges, tourists and local artists gave the connected cities of Houghton and Hancock an attractive refinement. Some of it even trickled out into the four-corner towns like the one her mother lived near. But not much. "Yeah, right."

He looked offended. "I'm serious. During the peak of its mining day, this area was a draw for actors and playwrights from as far as the East Coast."

"Thanks for the history lesson, Dr. Stahl, but I learned all that in school. Houghton and Hancock are just a couple of college towns separated by a pretty river."

She patted his arm, but quickly pulled back when she felt his muscle flex beneath her touch. "Nice try, though."

Jack looked at his arm before glancing back at her. "Can I help?"

She grabbed a carton of eggs, ignoring the brief tension that had materialized between them. "You can do the toast."

"Let me guess, you need nightlife and excitement. Noise."

She laughed. "I'm usually home by eight most nights and in bed by ten, real exciting."

Her cell phone rang. She pulled it out of the pocket of her sweats and answered. "This is Laura."

Her assistant gave her a message from Mr. Albertson about an invitation to a team-building retreat. Her manager RSVP'd for her to attend and Cindy sent her the details via email.

Laura would check her BlackBerry later. She continued making breakfast while getting office updates and then finally disconnected.

"She's calling you on Sunday morning?" Jack looked shocked.

Laura shrugged. "Sometimes we work weekends to catch up. No big deal."

"And I thought I worked hard." Jack slipped two pieces of bread into the toaster.

"Were you never on call for a weekend?"

"Well, yeah."

"See, no difference." Laura dumped scrambled eggs into a hot skillet.

"So, why the long face?" Jack asked.

She shook her head. "It's nothing, really."

"You miss it," Jack said.

She looked into his eyes. Big mistake. His gaze held understanding. "I've been home a week and I'm itching to get back."

The toast popped up and Jack buttered it. "What do you like most about your job?"

It was a good place to hide. With sales, everything was superficial. Laura didn't have to make people happy, just meet their business needs by offering a fair contract of service. Her job gave her confidence, a sense of importance. Like she counted for something. "It's something I do well."

"Better than making macaroni, I hope." His blue eyes twinkled.

If he was trying to flirt with her, he might as well give up. "Wait till you try the eggs. Should I call your daughter?"

"She's not much of a breakfast eater. If you don't mind, I'll let her sleep until after I shower."

"Sounds like a plan." Laura sat down and focused on her plate. She grabbed a piece of bacon and bit into it. "Mmm. Gotta love grease."

Jack's head was bowed. He really did the whole prayer thing before meals. He looked up at her and smiled.

The strip of bacon hung between her lips. She pushed it in and mumbled, "Sorry."

He waved her apology aside. "So tell me, what are business solutions?"

"Information system technology, network support, long-range planning, programming help, that sort of thing." She wiped her greasy fingers on a napkin.

Jack looked blank.

"Your vet practice had to have a computer."

He took a piece of toast. "We had a few, but I didn't get involved with them."

"What about a home PC?" Laura asked.

"The kids use it mostly. I rarely get online. I'm more of a paper kind of guy."

Laura grinned. "You're so outdated."

"So I've been told."

Laura laughed.

Jack liked the sound. Her laugh was full and strong, like she meant it. They chatted comfortably enough. Well, sort of. Even though she'd dressed in sweats, her hair was sleep-tousled. And he was crazy for noticing.

He polished off the last piece of bacon and stood, ready to clear the table. "I'm going to check out that apartment shower."

Laura looked up at him, her eyes wide and sweet. "Leave it. I can clean up."

He knew the sooner he left the better.

"Do you need a towel?" she blurted, her cheeks flushed. "Until you find yours, that is—I mean, until you unpack."

"I'm all set. I'll be back in awhile to get Ange."

Laura followed him toward the door. "Jack?"

He felt his heart trip over itself at the question in her voice. He turned.

"I was thinking—until you get settled in—Angie can stay here in the house while you get your things arranged."

He cocked his head. That wasn't a bad idea, but he didn't want Angie getting used to the space. She'd have to give it up eventually for the tiny loft. It might make things that much harder.

"Only if you're comfortable with it. One or two nights, tops." Her brow furrowed, as if she thought his hesitation had something to do with her.

"I don't want Angie getting in your way. Once she sets up camp, there'd be no booting her out." He tried to coax a smile back on her face. He got the feeling that she might be scared to stay alone in this big old house and that made no sense. It also blurred the confident image he had of her.

"Maybe she could use a little space right now."

That was probably true, too. Either way, he needed to check with Angie. "I'll let you know. Thanks for breakfast."

"It's one of the few meals I can handle," Laura said.

"Next time, let me cook." He could have kicked himself. She hadn't invited him for a next time. He didn't want her to, did he?

Her eyes held a challenge. "What's your specialty?"

"I have many, but wait till you try my pancakes." He gave her a wink and left.

Laura quickly showered and dressed, not bothering with makeup. She passed the closed door to where Angie still slept. The kid could snooze.

In the kitchen, Laura filled the sink with hot water and soap and dirty breakfast dishes. Looking out the window, she spotted a group of deer grazing in the field when a quick knock at the door startled her.

Jack stepped into the kitchen. His damp hair curled at the ends and he'd shaved. He looked great.

"Is she up yet?" Jack asked.

Laura found her voice. "Not yet."

"I'll get her moving. We've got work to do."

She waved him inside. "Go on up."

Looking uneasy, he walked past her into the dining room then charged up the stairs.

A few minutes later another knock at the door caught her attention.

Aunt Nelda entered with a box of doughnuts and a singsong voice. "Good morning. I thought I'd welcome the new neighbors."

Laura dried her hands. She heard Jack's footsteps coming down the stairs. Her aunt did, too.

With one eyebrow raised, Aunt Nelda asked, "Did I come at a bad time?"

"No." She peered inside the doughnut box. Why'd she feel like she'd just been caught snitching a cookie?

Jack entered the kitchen.

Aunt Nelda stared at Jack.

He stared back.

Looking confused and maybe even a little hurt, Aunt Nelda glanced from Laura's wet head to Jack's.

Even though Laura's cheeks blazed, she looked her aunt straight in the eye. "This is Jack Stahl, the new neighbor. And this is my aunt, Nelda Scott."

Aunt Nelda's eyes narrowed.

Jack extended his hand, but the tips of his ears were red. "Ms. Scott."

Her aunt shook his hand firmly.

"The power was out, so I asked Jack and his daughter to stay here for the night instead of trying to unpack in the dark."

"Ah." The confusion cleared from her aunt's brow. "It stormed pretty hard last night."

Angie appeared in a pair of jeans and T-shirt.

"And this is Jack's daughter, Angie," Laura said. "My aunt Nelda."

Angie slipped into a chair at the table. "Hi."

"She brought doughnuts. I'll make more coffee," Laura said quickly.

"I'll do that, you ladies sit," Jack said.

That brought up both of her aunt's eyebrows. "You know your way around a kitchen."

"It's just coffee," he said.

Laura pushed the box of doughnuts toward Angie. "You get first pick."

"My, my, a man who cooks is worth his weight in gold." Subtlety was foreign to Aunt Nelda.

Laura looked at Angie. "Want milk?"

Angie nodded. She had powdered sugar all over her lips.

When the coffee finished brewing, Jack filled three mugs and sat down. "So, Ms. Scott, do you live near here?"

"Oh, no. I live in an exclusive subdivision in Houghton." The lilt in her aunt's voice clearly implied that she lived in *the* place to live. Aunt Nelda smoothed her hair. Her rings sparkled.

Laura glanced at Angie. The poor kid needed something to lighten the moment, so Laura crossed her eyes.

Angie sputtered powdered sugar all over the table.

Laura snickered.

"Ange," Jack warned.

"She made me laugh," Angie said.

"It wasn't me." Laura jumped up for a dishcloth, but she grinned at Angie.

Jack stood. "Come on, Ange. Let's get to work unpacking."

The sweet light in Angie's eyes went out. She got up from the table with about as much enthusiasm as she might rally for a dentist appointment.

"It was very nice to meet you, Ms. Scott," Jack said at the door. He waited for Angie, who dillydallied putting her glass in the sink.

"Yes. And you must call me Aunt Nelda."

Aunt Nelda didn't invite just anyone to address her as family.

Once Jack and Angie were safely out the door and on the porch, Aunt Nelda whispered, "He's perfect for you."

"What?"

Aunt Nelda smiled. "He kept looking at you."

Laura flushed. "You're seeing things."

Her aunt looked very pleased. "See, I told you God's in control."

"Let's hope He has control when it comes to telling Mom the barn sold," Laura muttered. She cleared the table and wrapped up the leftover doughnuts, but her aunt's words echoed through her thoughts.

He's perfect for you.

Jack Stahl was nice and handsome, but he had two teenagers. Besides, she didn't want to stay and play house. Laura wanted that promotion. As soon as her mom was back on her feet, she'd head back to Wisconsin and that'd be the end of the attraction.

Chapter Six

It was just a dream.

Jack rubbed his eyes, and then checked the clock on his bedside table. Seven-fifteen. He lay back against his pillow and reached next to him, finding empty space. No wife.

He'd stopped reaching for his wife shortly after her death, but this morning, he'd dreamed of Joanne. He woke expecting to find her next to him with her dark hair spread across her pillow. A needle-sharp pang of regret shot through him as he stared at his only window.

The red-and-white checked curtains fluttered in the breeze. His new home was little more than a studio apartment. Knotty-pine walls and wide-plank floors gave the place a simple rustic quality he found appealing. But stuffy. With only one window, he couldn't get a cross-circulation of air and the back of his neck was damp with sweat.

He couldn't move Angie into the loft until he installed a window. She'd roast if he didn't. He'd have to let Angie stay another night in the big house with Laura. An image of Laura in her pink sweats flashed through his mind.

"Lord, help me keep my thoughts on You today," he muttered.

He wandered across the bare floor to his kitchen and made

coffee. Tempted to go back to bed, he checked his list of things to do. Too many items hadn't been crossed off but building Angie a window took top priority.

With a cup of coffee in hand, Jack read through his Bible passages and prayed. It was after eight when he finally stepped onto Laura's porch to leave a note about running errands. The house remained quiet. Angie and Laura were no doubt asleep, which was just as well. He'd rather not see Laura this morning. Not when he missed his wife.

Laura entered the kitchen to a flood of morning sunlight filtering through the dotted Swiss café curtains. She watched dust motes dance in the sunbeams until she noticed a folded piece of paper lying on the floor. Opening it, she read the scratch of Jack's handwriting and laid it on the table for Angie.

Angie entered the kitchen, her fuzzy slippers scuffing along the linoleum floor.

"There's a note from your dad. He went to the hardware store."

Angie flipped it open.

Scooping coffee into the machine, Laura asked, "Want some cereal?"

"Sure." Angie yawned.

"Thanks for picking up milk on your way back from dinner last night with your dad. Did you two have a good time?"

"It was okay." Something was on the kid's mind, Laura could tell.

"Would you like to take a walk around the property before I go to the hospital?"

Angie shrugged. "I guess."

Did she have a fight with Jack? "Are you okay?"

Angie kept stirring her cereal instead of eating it. She dropped her spoon against her bowl. "It's just weird."

"What is?"

"Being here. I mean, it's so quiet and—I dunno."

"It doesn't feel like home?" Laura sat down.

Angie slumped against her chair, her cereal forgotten.

"It'll get better," Laura said.

"When?"

"After you've been to school and made some friends. Let's just say by Thanksgiving." Laura poured herself a bowl of cereal.

Angie didn't look convinced.

"Change is hard, but it can be good, too." She'd used that line a few times with clients, but Angie wasn't biting.

Bleak discouragement shone from Angie's blue eyes. "You sound like my dad."

"Do I?"

"For months he's been blabbing about change until I was ready to puke."

Laura didn't blame Angie for thinking her world had been put into a blender on high speed. Why Jack dragged his daughter to this isolated area was beyond her. "So, did you?"

"Did I what?"

"Puke?"

Angie actually giggled. "No."

"Your dad loves you, so maybe you should give him a little grace on this one."

"Grace?"

"You know, controlled patience. In five years you'll be off to college like your brother. And trust me, it's easier on your own if you've been toughened up a little at home."

She had Angie's attention. "What do you mean?"

For a moment, Laura panicked. She didn't know what Angie needed, but she knew what loneliness felt like. As a kid, Laura had to entertain herself and stay out of her mother's way in the process.

With a deep breath, Laura stood. "Watch carefully, because this is straight out of sales training. In a difficult situation, instead of letting on that you're rattled, you stay in control beautifully."

She walked across the kitchen with her head held high then bowed gracefully before Angie.

The kid giggled.

"See, no sulking. Maintain posture. They teach this at Miss America pageants, too." Laura knew a tough sale when she saw one. Her forte with clients was not appearing too eager or coming on too strong. She'd give Angie that same treatment. The girl looked like she could use a friend.

"Were you ever in a beauty pageant?" Angie asked quietly.

"No, but I practiced in the living room until I was your age. My mother never knew how to handle my dress-up stage. She used to say I was acting foolish."

Angie smiled in understanding.

"So, what do you like to do?" Laura asked.

Angie looked thoughtful. "I dunno."

"Sports, school, boys, cheerleading—what are you looking to do here?"

Angie smiled. "I wouldn't mind being a cheerleader. And my dad promised to buy me a horse."

Laura's eyes widened. *Good move, Jack.* "Do you ride, then?"

"A little. I used to take lessons."

"What happened?"

"I used to go with my mom." Angie looked down at her cereal bowl.

"Oh." Laura clenched her teeth. Great, she'd just reminded the poor girl of her dead mother.

Laura opened her phone. "Do you mind if I make a couple quick phone calls?"

Angie shrugged. "Go ahead."

Laura checked her work voice mail. She forwarded the ones Cindy could work on and made a note to deal with the others later.

She dialed another number. "Hello, Mom? I've got a few things to do here before I come to the hospital. I'll see you later this afternoon. Okay?"

"When's your mom coming home?" Angie put her bowl in the sink.

"In a couple of days."

"What about your dad?" Angie asked.

"He died when I was your age." Laura took in Angie's surprise.

"Really? Did he have a stroke, too?"

"No. He worked in a plastics company. There was a chemical leak that caused lethal fumes. They had to evacuate, but my dad had already inhaled too much. He died before they reached the hospital. My mom and I didn't say goodbye." Laura swallowed hard.

"I didn't get to say anything to my mom, either. She died in Colorado." Angie's eyes were dull, lifeless.

Laura quietly asked, "You want to talk about it?"

Angie sniffed and wiped her nose on her sleeve. "At least you get it."

"Yeah, I get it," Laura said.

Angie ran her finger through the cereal dust on the table. "My mom died while she and my dad where on vacation."

Laura's gut twisted. How terrible for Jack. What he must have gone through—they all went through. She held her breath, forcing herself to wait for Angie to tell more, if she wanted to. The kid looked like she needed to.

"Mom didn't want to go, but my dad took her white-water rafting on the Colorado River." Angie flipped her long braid off her shoulder. Her voice was flat, emotionless. "Their raft tipped over and my mom hit her head. She had a helmet on, but it didn't help. She died in the hospital before my brother and I could get there."

Laura's heart ached hearing the story. She could just imagine the guilt Jack must feel. And Angie blamed her dad. What a mess! "I'm so sorry."

Angie shrugged.

"Have you talked to your dad about how you feel?" Laura winced. It was such an adult thing to say.

Angie stiffened. A clear sign the conversation was over. "There's nothing I can say that will bring Mom back, so what's the use?"

Laura squeezed Angie's shoulder. "Well, if you ever need to unload, I'm a good listener."

"Thanks." Angie looked relieved that Laura wasn't going to pry.

It dawned on Laura that Jack had moved to get rid of the weight that hung around his daughter's heart. Maybe even to exorcise the painful memories steeped in their old home. It took more than a new location to heal. A person couldn't erase the hurt that way. A person couldn't relocate heartbreak or disappointment. Scars had a way of sticking around, even after they'd faded.

"You know, Angie, it's okay to miss our parents. It helps us remember the good things about them. And one of the things my dad loved was this property. What do you say we take a walk and look for blackberries? I'm pretty sure they're ready to pick."

Angie looked surprised by the invitation. "I'll go change."

"I'll get the berry buckets."

Laura entered the hospital room. Still the only occupant, her mother watched what she wanted on television and cranked the volume until it blared. "Can we turn this down?"

Her mom, sitting in a chair, used the remote with her good hand. "The doctor says I can go home in a day or two."

"I know. He said you'd still need physical therapy for a while. Three times a week."

Her mom looked at her. "I don't know who's going to take me. I can't drive all that way."

"I'll take you until we hire a health aide who can do the exercises with you at home. That way you won't have to come into Hancock." And Laura could return to work.

Her mother shrugged. "What took you so long to get here?"

I was picking berries with a girl who's devastated like I was.
Laura took a deep breath and clicked off the TV. "Mom, I have
to tell you something."

Her mom's eyelids were puffy and loose skin hung under
her chin. She looked so old.

Laura dropped her gaze. "I sold the barn and twenty acres."

Surprise washed across her mom's features. "To who?"

"A guy named Jack Stahl and his thirteen-year-old daughter.
He's a veterinarian who's buying out Dr. Walter's practice.
Jack wants to eventually move the practice into Daddy's barn.
With work, it'd be the perfect setup. Jack's son is a freshman
at Michigan Tech. You'll like them." Laura watched her mom
digest the news.

"It'll be nice to have someone nearby, in case of emergencies."

Laura's jaw clenched. Her mother never missed an opportunity to make her feel bad about leaving home. But when
Laura came home, her mother acted like she was in the way.

Her mom turned and looked straight through her. "Don't
ever get old, Laura."

"Are you sure you're okay with this?"

"Laura, I've thought about selling the barn since you went
away to college. But I never could bring myself to do it. It
wasn't your idea, so don't worry about it."

Laura nodded. "You know me. I've got to have something
to stew about."

"It's the Toivo way," her mom said with a rare attempt at humor.

"You got that right." Laura breathed easier. Maybe everything was going to work out like Aunt Nelda said.

Laura drove home with a couple of large pizzas stacked on
the passenger seat. The aroma tempted her to sneak a slice, but
she'd wait. She'd called Jack's cell to ask if they'd had dinner.
He'd sounded surprised, even grateful. He accepted her offer

on the condition that she'd eat dinner at his place so he and Angie could show off what they'd done to the apartment.

Walking toward the side door of the barn, Laura squelched the anticipation that raced up her spine. She was looking forward to seeing Angie. That was all.

She stepped into the barn and the sweet aroma of baked goods mingled with the scent of pizza. She knocked on the door to the apartment.

"Come in," Jack yelled.

"What is that incredible smell?"

"We baked you a blackberry pie," Angie said. She set the table with paper plates and napkins.

Laura glanced at Jack who wore oven mitts on both hands. He was dressed in old jeans and a T-shirt. He pulled the pie out of the little oven and rested it on the counter. Steam poured out of the top of the crust.

She set the pizza boxes on the kitchen table then stepped close to the counter and breathed in deeply. "Wow."

Angie peeked into each box. "Ugh, mushrooms."

"Just pick them off," Jack said.

Angie gave him an annoyed look, but they'd worked together to bake a pie—for her. Why?

Before she forgot, Laura reached inside her purse and pulled out a key. She handed it to Jack. "I had it made. In case you need to get into the house."

His eyes widened. "I'm not comfortable with that. I mean, what's your mom going to think?"

"Exactly the reason I want you to have a key. Just in case, you know, after I'm gone."

He took the key from her fingers.

Laura didn't care for the way her skin tingled from the connection. She stepped back, making a show of looking around. The wood floors gleamed and the walls did, too. "You've done a lot in a short time."

"Thanks. I think a few area rugs will help, and Angie needs new linens for the bunk beds in the loft, but otherwise we're in good shape."

She looked up. Sunlight shined inside making shadows against the ceiling fan.

"I'm putting in a window," Jack said.

She saw the stacked lumber and toolbox near the spiral staircase. "It'll brighten this place up."

"Of course, it's going slower than I anticipated."

Angie pointed to the loft. "There's a ton of saw dust all over."

Laura understood. "Angie can stay another night if you need her to."

"Can I, Dad?"

"One more night, then we'll get your bedroom set up." Jack washed his hands at the sink.

Laura noticed the slump of Angie's shoulders. Was it the space of Laura's old room? Or did Angie feel more grown up staying under another roof? It couldn't be because of her, could it?

"Come on, let's eat." Jack's voice scattered her thoughts.

After a brief dinner prayer, they dug into the pizza in silence. Laura felt awkward in their apartment, like she didn't belong there. The small space felt too intimate, cozy.

"Don't forget, we've got dessert," Angie said with a lilt to her voice.

Laura groaned. "You know, I'm feeling pretty special about this pie and I think it deserves a special time. I can't just scarf it down after all that pizza. I want to savor every piece. Can you and your dad bring it over a little later? I have ice cream in the freezer."

Angie looked skeptical.

But Laura needed to make her escape. This felt like they were a little family. Laura wasn't comfortable with family— they expected too much.

Jack came to her rescue. Maybe he felt the same vibes, since he'd been awfully quiet. "We'll see you in an hour or so."

"Perfect. Is that okay, Angie?" Laura said.

"What kind of ice cream do you have?"

Laura scanned Jack's kitchenette. The half-sized fridge didn't have much of a freezer. The counter space was limited and the oven small, but they still managed to bake her a pie. "Vanilla. If you'd like, you can store as much ice cream as you want in Mom's freezer."

Jack laughed. "Don't worry. I have a chest freezer I haven't set up yet. We'll be fine, but thanks for the offer."

"See you in a bit."

Back at the house, Laura laid her purse on the kitchen table and called her aunt to tell her how her mom had taken the news. Then she popped open her laptop. The house felt empty again.

Laura had fancied her mother's house as a living thing that missed her. And maybe that's why she didn't like staying alone within its walls. With second floor windows that resembled a pair of eyes, the house reminded Laura too much of what she'd once wanted—a warm and loving family of her own.

Jack knocked and peeked his head inside the screen door. Laura sat at the kitchen table with her laptop. It looked like she was poring over a serious spreadsheet. Not his idea of fun. She didn't look pleased, either. A frown marred her pretty face. "Ready for pie?"

She brightened when she saw him. "More than ever."

He checked the clock over the kitchen table. "Mind if we watch *Jeopardy?*"

Laura's eyes widened. "You're kidding, right?"

"My dad's a freak," Angie whispered.

Jack coughed. "Uh, I can hear you."

Laura clicked *Save* and closed the laptop. "My mother's going to love you. Heaven forbid, she ever missed Alex Trebek. We can eat in the living room."

Angie did the honor of slicing and serving the pie with mounds of vanilla ice cream.

Jack reached for his plate and headed for the couch and the TV. He couldn't get over how Angie had connected with Laura. She'd badgered him to get over here when Jack knew Laura needed space. Having her over for dinner in the apartment had been odd. Comfortable, yet strained. He still couldn't figure it out. Still, Angie came to life around Laura. For that, he'd sacrifice his comfort zone. Besides, he owed Laura more than just dessert. She'd helped soothe the sting of moving.

"Mmm. Incredible. Might even be better than my mom's." Laura's eyes closed when she took a bite.

Angie glanced at him with pride. "Hear that, Dad? Pretty good for our first pie."

"Yup."

They'd followed one of Joanne's recipes. She'd been an amazing cook. He was grateful she'd kept such good notes. He'd had to use her recipes a lot these last two years. Joanne had been a good homemaker. A good wife. He'd taken so much for granted, putting his practice first and rushing through life. He thought she'd always be there.

During a commercial, he turned toward Laura who sat in a cushioned rocking chair. "How's your mom?"

"She's getting stronger with physical therapy, and it looks like her blood pressure has finally stabilized. I warn you, she's not the warm and fuzzy type, but she likes the idea of having neighbors."

"Calling her Mom's probably not a good idea." Jack shoveled in the last of his pie.

Laura laughed. "She might think you'd bought more than the barn."

Jack felt his gut tighten. Pushing the boundaries of his acquaintance with Laura was dangerous. A disaster waiting to happen. Laura wasn't interested in slowing down to concentrate on family. Hadn't she said as much when she explained how much she missed her work? He didn't dare alienate Angie by getting romantically involved with a woman she looked up to. It'd never work. And yet, here he sat watching TV next to Laura.

After another show, Jack rose to leave. The fading light of an evening sun fused through the windows, casting rosy shadows against the walls. "I think we're in for a great sunset, ladies."

Laura peered out the window. "We can watch it from the porch."

Angie stood and yawned. "I'm going to bed."

Jack looked closely at his daughter before kissing the top of her head. "You feeling okay?"

Angie rolled her eyes. "I'm just tired. Good night, Dad."

He chuckled. It'd been a long day. "Night, honey."

He followed Laura onto the porch with every intention of leaving for his apartment. "Thanks for taking Angie to pick berries, and taking an interest in her."

"She's a great girl. You did a nice job." Laura sat on the bench swing.

He leaned against one of the posts. He'd been at work so much of the time, he didn't feel right taking credit. "Mostly my wife's doing. I didn't get home until late most nights."

Laura bit her bottom lip. "Angie told me what happened, how Joanne died. I'm so sorry."

"She talked about it?"

Laura nodded.

"She doesn't talk about it to anyone. Not Ben, our minister, my sister, not even her friends that I know of. She locked it away."

He knew girls tended to bond quicker with each other. Lord only knew how badly Jack had tried to take Joanne's place only to be shut down time and again. Being a mom was not a role designed for him. Angie needed the influence of a woman, especially at this age. A friend in Laura could really help his daughter.

"She'll come around, Jack."

Jack looked into Laura's eyes and felt trapped there. "I owe you more than blackberry pie."

Laura shook her head. "You don't owe me a thing. Maybe I relate to Angie because I lost my dad when I was her age. I understand what she's going through. But, how'd you do it, Jack? How do you deal with the grief?"

He looked at the sun laying low on the horizon. Not an easy question. "I have an eternal hope. Joanne did, too."

"Be really good and go to heaven?"

He faced her, the sunset completely forgotten. "Heaven's not something you earn, Laura. Lord knows I wouldn't make the grade. Hope of an eternity with God allows me to look differently at death. It doesn't take away the grief, or my part in it, but it does remove the finality of it."

"You believe you'll see her again." Her voice was low, cautious, questioning.

"I do."

"What if you remarry?"

He ran a hand through his hair. It was something he wanted someday, but not now. There was too much at stake with Angie. "I think relationships will be different in heaven. More spiritual."

Laura nodded. "Interesting."

"I loved my wife, but becoming a vet had always seemed more important. I went overboard with study, volunteer work and building my partnership. I kind of missed the whole quality-time thing with my family."

She didn't look like she believed him. "But you're so good with Angie."

"I'm trying to recapture some of the carefree spirit of my youth. Only the good parts, mind you. Angie needs to see that I'm not all work and no play. This place and you are helping me to do that."

"Me?" Her wide eyes reflected surprise.

"No pressure or anything, but my daughter likes you. She doesn't warm up to just anyone."

Her brow furrowed as if she didn't trust his words, his confidence in her. "Thanks, Jack, but I don't know much about kids."

"You seem to know what Angie needs, and for that I'm grateful."

"I don't know what to say." She didn't look away.

The warmth shining from her eyes gave him courage. He didn't want to overwhelm her, but he had to ask. "You might say that you'll continue to help Angie. Be her friend."

And help him, too, but he didn't want to push it. He had to be careful with Laura.

Chapter Seven

The scent of brewing coffee coaxed Laura awake. She heard the soft mumble of voices downstairs and smiled. She could get used to Jack and Angie in the kitchen. She stretched her arms overhead and threw back the covers.

Laura had thought about how real God was for Jack. Jack didn't wear his beliefs like a pair of Sunday trousers left in the closet the rest of the week. His faith had sustained him through the loss of his wife, the troubles with his daughter, and life in general. Jack had confidence in more than just himself.

He trusted her with his daughter after only a few days. Anthony had dated her for years, and she'd never felt this level of assurance. It was nice. It was also scary. What if she messed up? What if she came between Angie and her father? She couldn't refuse his plea for help, but she'd still tread with care.

Throwing on a pair of jeans and a T-shirt, she headed downstairs. The sweet smells wafting from the kitchen had her mouth watering by the time she reached the bottom step. She headed straight for the coffee pot. "Morning."

Jack turned from the stove. "I hope you don't mind us using your kitchen. I promised you my specialty and thought it'd be easier to cook them over here."

Laura smiled. "You two are spoiling me rotten."

"Do you want blackberries in your pancakes?" Angie asked. She worked beside Jack, poking her dad with her elbow for more room. Jack only crowded closer. They seemed to be getting along just fine.

Laura peeked at the pools of pancake batter bubbling on the stove and breathed in deep. "I'm going to be fat by the time I leave."

Jack grinned. "You don't cook much, do you?"

Three was definitely a crowd at her mother's stovetop. Laura backed away before she did something crazy like gather them close. "I order takeout."

"Don't you eat anything healthy?" Jack asked.

"I like salads." Laura leaned her hip against the counter while Angie arranged plates and silverware on the table. Cradling her mug of coffee with both hands, Laura sipped just as Jack reached into the cupboard above her.

She spotted a glass that wobbled. She went after it just as Jack moved. She collided into his shoulder, sloshing her coffee. She managed to catch the glass with one hand and pinned it against Jack's arm to keep it steady.

"You got it?" Jack's eyes twinkled.

Laura set her mug down, feeling like she played Twister against the kitchen counter. Her heart beat an erratic rhythm that had everything to do how Jack's eyes had darkened as he looked at her.

He had lines across his forehead and bits of gray hiding in the dark blond of his hair. He didn't move a muscle, but the twitch to his lips clued her in that he'd picked up on the effect his nearness had on her.

"You going to put the glass down or what?"

The urge to step closer made Laura pause. Just what would Jack do if she did? Instead, she squared her shoulders and stepped back. "I'll put it on the table."

Laura glanced at Angie. Had the girl picked up on the attraction that sparked between her and Jack?

"Dad," Angie warned. "The pancakes need to be flipped and I don't want to ruin them."

"One of these days, Ange, you're going to have to learn how to flip a cake like your daddy."

"You make them too big." But Angie inched closer to the stove.

Laura watched Angie play the mama bear protecting her cub, putting her body between her dad and unseen danger. Brooke had done it countless times at Anthony's. She'd squeeze between them on the couch when they'd rent a movie, or break their handhold so she could take each of their hands. Laura had learned her lesson, never come between a daughter and her dad.

Still, the close encounter with Jack left Laura feeling prickly. Laura wasn't about to get stuck playing house in the U.P. the rest of her life. She'd wanted that once, but she didn't think she was cut out for such a role. She yearned for a promotion that would take her far from home for weeks on end. The exhilarating challenge of negotiating bigger contracts beckoned. She wasn't about to miss that opportunity. It'd give her life new meaning. Success.

She glanced at Jack. A good man, but one better left alone. Having Jack Stahl would be like winning the lottery—a fat chance and life altering to boot. But would such a chance prove positive or negative? Laura wasn't about to take risks with her heart. She'd done that before and lost.

Jack looked away from Laura and stared at the griddle. He felt like the pancakes he flipped. Hot and rough around the edges. "Thanks, Ange. Another minute and they'd be trash."

He wished his daughter had been anywhere but in the kitchen this morning. Fortunately, his brain had kicked in before he did something he'd regret.

He'd be insane to start something with an ambitious woman like Laura Toivo. He knew the signs of a workaholic. He'd been there, done that. It was hard to compete with that work-till-you-drop high. He'd placed work before Joanne and the kids, and he'd never put himself or his family through that again. Not with anyone.

"Here's the first batch." Jack slipped a stack of pancakes onto a plate. He poured more batter into pools on the griddle.

"Let Laura have them," his daughter said with a smile.

Jack handed over the plate. "The key is a load of butter."

He watched Laura drizzle her stack with syrup and then take her first bite. He grit his teeth when her eyes closed in obvious bliss.

"How are they?" Jack finally said. "If they're tough, I've got more."

Laura wiped a drop of syrup from her bottom lip. Her mouth full, she nodded and mumbled, "Good."

"Ange." Jack tossed two cakes onto her plate. He sat down with his own plateful and briefly closed his eyes before digging in.

"You didn't *pray*," Laura said.

"How do you know?" He looked at Angie who rolled her eyes.

"You didn't bow your head."

"Sometimes a man needs to pray silently," he said.

"Oh." Laura returned to her pancakes with vigor.

Conversation ceased to the sounds of forks scraping against the plates, but Jack still felt the pull. The air crackled with unseen energy and awareness.

"Can we go shopping today?" Angie blurted.

Jack was grateful for a diversion but cringed. She'd been after him about new school clothes for weeks. It wasn't a pastime he enjoyed. "We've got your stuff to unpack, and the loft to clean."

Angie slouched her head back and groaned. "You promised you'd take me before school starts."

He had. But he hated shopping. Without thinking, he glanced at Laura. Women liked that sort of thing. If he hinted, would she volunteer? Was that taking advantage of her agreement to help out?

"You know, Jack, Angie could come with me to the hospital, if you don't mind her meeting my mom. We could hit a few stores afterward and be back before dinner."

He gave Angie a wink. "You don't mind carting my daughter around? She can be pretty fussy."

Laura smiled. "I haven't shopped here in ages. It'd be fun."

He could finish painting the loft windowsill and get a host of other things done. He reached for his wallet and pulled out five twenties. "What do you think, Ange. Is that enough?"

"I'd double it. Better yet, don't you have a credit card?" Laura said.

Angie placed her arm on the table with her palm open while she smiled at Laura.

After a brief hesitation, Jack handed over his card. One problem solved. He only hoped a new one wouldn't be born. Angie flashing plastic.

"Thanks, Dad."

Laura put her dish in the sink. "I'm going to shower, but don't you dare touch those dishes. I'll clean up before we leave."

Jack waited until he knew Laura was out of hearing range before he turned toward Angie. "You don't mind if Laura takes you?"

Angie fingered the credit card with a grin. "Works better this way."

Jack groaned. "Be careful with that. Just because you have my card doesn't mean you can go hog wild."

His daughter rolled her eyes. "I won't."

He pulled on her braid. "Keep your eyes peeled for a new bedspread and curtains for your room. See if Laura will help you pick out the colors. She's probably good at that stuff. And don't lose my card."

Angie nodded. Without complaint, she helped him stack the

dishes in the sink and wipe off the table. Then she charged up the stairs to get ready for her shopping spree.

Jack savored the last of his coffee. He might actually have his daughter back.

"Mom?" Laura peeked into the hospital room. "I brought you a visitor."

Her mother sat in the high-backed chair dressed in a pair of lavender sweats that looked like an Aunt Nelda cast-off. Her hair was combed and she'd applied a sweep of blush. "Who?"

Laura opened the door wide. "This is Angie Stahl, your new neighbor."

"My, my, hello there." Her mother's eyes softened.

Angie stepped forward. "Hi, Mrs. Ti-Toi-vo," she stammered.

"Oh no, you must call me Anna." Her mother gave Ange the same smile she gave Nancy's kids. It made Laura's heart hitch. She might never give her mother grandkids and that'd be a shame. Laura liked this softer side of her mother.

"Are you ready to start school?" her mom asked.

Angie gave Laura a grin. "I haven't been school shopping yet."

"We're going after we leave here," Laura said.

Her mom nodded. "I know how important clothes are for school. I won't keep you. We have good schools here with lots of nice kids. A pretty girl like you will make friends in no time."

Laura smiled at her mom. It was a nice thing to say, and absolutely true. Angie promised to be a beauty.

"Laura and I picked blackberries yesterday."

Her mother looked at Laura wide-eyed. "I'm surprised she remembered where to find them."

Laura winced at the subtle slam. "I love picking berries."

"So did your father. But they must be overgrown by now."

Laura remembered gathering bucketfuls with her dad. She'd kept it up through her teen years in order to supply her mother ample berries for jam. She missed having that jam. How long had it been since her mother made any? "We found a pretty good spot."

Angie smiled. "Some of them were as big as my thumb."

Laura's mom nodded. "Well, you can pick them any time, Angie."

"Thanks, Mrs. Toivo."

After a few awkward moments of silence, Laura cleared her throat. "Sorry, Mom, but we're losing prime shopping time."

Angie turned to leave, but Laura's mom grabbed her hand. "Thank you for coming to visit me."

Angie took it all in stride by covering the older woman's hand with her own. "You're welcome."

Laura leaned down and kissed her mother's forehead. "I'll see you tomorrow."

Jack dialed his cell phone. "Hello, Laura?"

"Hi, Jack. Sorry we're running late. We're in line at Wal-Mart. Angie picked out a nice set of twin quilts for her bunk beds and matching curtains and a rug. They'll brighten up—"

He cut her off. "Great. Listen. Can you drop Angie off at the Chinese restaurant in Houghton in half an hour? Ben called and he wants to meet us for dinner."

"The one on Main Street?"

"That's the one."

"We'll be there." Click. She hung up.

Jack rested his cell phone against his chin. He hadn't invited Laura to join them. Would she assume she was welcome or back off? He wasn't opposed to her presence. It'd be nice to introduce her to Ben. But everything depended on Angie. If she had a rough time, he'd know.

It was up to Angie to invite Laura to stay.

Laura could not remember the last time she'd had this much fun shopping. She'd put Angie through her paces and the girl thrived under the attention. Laura knew her candid opinions buoyed Angie's confidence. Thank goodness Jack had let her take his daughter. At this age, Angie needed a woman's input when it came to clothes.

Thirty-five minutes after Jack had called, they rushed into the restaurant loaded with rustling shopping bags. She hoped Jack approved of the trendy jeans and tops. They were awfully cute on his daughter's tall, thin frame.

Scanning the crowded tables, Laura spotted Jack sitting with a younger version of himself—his son, Ben. Both men stood as they approached.

"Did you buy the place out?" Jack asked.

"Almost," Angie said with a giggle.

Laura handed Jack the receipts for Angie's purchases along with his credit card. "I had to sign your name a few times." She turned toward his son. "You must be Ben. I'm Laura Toivo."

Ben was taller than his father and his hair was longer, lighter blond, and had more waves. He was adorable and by the width of his smile, he knew it. "Dad's told me a lot about you. Thanks for taking care of the runt."

"Hey!" Angie backhanded her brother's chest.

Ben pulled her hair.

"Ouch!" Angie growled.

"It's my pleasure." Laura slipped her purse onto her shoulder. "Well, I better get home. Nice to meet you, Ben."

"Wait." Angie stepped forward. "Aren't you going to eat dinner with us? Isn't Chinese one of your favorites?"

Laura felt her cheeks burn. She didn't want to intrude. Jack might wish to spend time with his kids alone. "It is, but you guys need to catch up."

"Come on, Laura," Ben said with a saucy wink. "Have dinner with us, Dad's buying."

She glanced at Jack, searching his eyes for a clue.

He pushed out the chair next to him with his foot.

She looked at Angie. The kid had this expectant anticipation in her eyes, like she wanted her to stay. It didn't help that the amazing scent of the food was killing Laura's willpower.

With a sigh, Laura sank into the chair Jack had offered. "You're not paying for mine."

"Yes, I am. It's the least I can do." His gaze held gratitude, and maybe something else. Something better left unnamed.

Laura looked away and grabbed a menu.

Ben sneaked one of Angie's shopping bags. "What'd you buy?"

Angie reached for it, but Ben held it out of her reach. "Dad!"

Ben pulled out the pair of jeans with embroidery along the cuff and calf of one leg followed by a dusty-rose peasant top. He whistled. "Wow, Ange. You're going to look like a real girl in this."

Angie rolled her eyes. "You're such a jerk."

"Your brother's trying to give you a compliment. And cool it with the eyes already. Ben, give her back her things."

Laura bit her lip to keep from smiling. Despite the sibling bickering, it was easy to recognize the closeness between them.

"Your sister's got good fashion sense," Laura said.

Ben's eyes narrowed. "Yeah, with your help."

"So?" Angie taunted.

"I'm just saying," Ben said.

Jack leaned close to Laura and whispered, "Thank you."

Laura ignored the shiver that raced through her. Her mind had gone blank the moment Jack moved toward her. Thankfully, his kids were bickering and didn't notice.

The waitress took their orders, bringing calm to the table once again. Laura turned to Ben. "What are you studying at school?"

"Engineering. I'm not sure what emphasis."

"Not interested in being a vet?" Laura asked.

Ben laughed. "No way. I'm allergic to dogs and cats, just like my mom. We never had real pets, just a hamster and some fish."

"You're kidding." Laura looked at Jack.

He shrugged. "It's true."

"Do you like dogs?" Angie asked.

"I love dogs, but I'm never home."

Angie's face fell.

"Hey, Runt, you were born in the Year of the Hare," Ben said. "See, it's a big rabbit. Must be why you can run fast."

When Jack pointed out his respective birth year animal from the Chinese calendar placemats, Laura blurted, "Wait, how old are you?"

"I turned thirty-seven in June."

"You must have married young," Laura said, quickly doing the math.

"Mom and Dad had to get married after high school," Angie said. "They were going to have Ben."

Laura glanced at Jack, her mouth slightly open. She didn't know what surprised her more, his age or the fact that he'd *had* to get married. She gave him credit for not hiding the reason from his kids.

"Now you've shocked her with the Stahl family secret." Jack gave her a lopsided grin.

The idea of Jack forced into marriage cracked his Mr. Wholesome image. That he'd stayed married spoke volumes about his character. "I'm impressed, Dr. Stahl. You worked through college with a wife and a baby. That's amazing."

"My father paid for my tuition." Jack shrugged off the compliment.

The food arrived, effectively shutting down conversation except for offers to try each other's meals. Laura laughed when Ben grimaced at her choice of moo shoo pork with Chinese pancakes.

"I love pancakes." Laura glanced at Jack.

He held her gaze a moment too long.

When the waitress came to clear plates, Laura covered hers with a protective hand. "To-go box, please."

Jack raised his eyebrow.

Laura grinned at Angie. "Midnight snack."

Angie smiled back.

They stepped away from the table, Angie charging ahead as Jack left cash for the bill.

She heard Ben's comment. "Way to go, Dad, she's like perfect."

Jack uttered a low bark of laughter. "Yeah, well, forget it. It'd never work."

The attraction was definitely mutual for Laura, but just as impossible. Laura wasn't looking to step into the role of anyone's stepmother. She'd tried out for that part before and got cut. She wasn't about to repeat an audition.

Still, it didn't mean she couldn't be a friend to both Jack and Angie. They'd moved next door to her mother, which meant they'd be a part of her mother's life. And Laura's, too, on occasion. Like Jack had said, it wouldn't work. They wanted different things. They were in different places in their lives.

Once outside, she waited with Angie near Jack's SUV for the guys to catch up.

"Thanks for dinner," Laura said.

"You're welcome." Jack pointed his key and the doors unlocked with a click.

Ben stretched. "Dad, can you give me a ride to the fairgrounds? Tonight's the last night of the carnival and I'm meeting friends there."

"What carnival?" Angie perked up.

"It's a couple blocks from the hospital."

"Can we go?" Angie asked.

Jack looked at Laura. "The evening's still young. Care to make a night of it?"

Laura hadn't been to the Houghton County Fair in years. As a kid, the fair had been the highlight of her summer and she wouldn't mind reliving a few good memories. Besides, she didn't relish an evening working on her laptop. Not on a warm summer night like this.

With a smile at Angie, she said, "Sure, why not?"

Chapter Eight

"Stay close to your brother," Jack told his daughter, who was anxious to catch up with Ben and his friends.

"*Okay*, Dad." Angie rolled her eyes.

"I mean it." Jack watched Ange race away. He didn't like the broad smile Angie gave Ben's roommate. It looked like Ben didn't, either. His son stepped between the two and playfully palmed Angie's head with a shove.

Ben had grown up since his mom's death. In many ways his son had slipped into Joanne's role as the family anchor. With sporting events and church functions, Ben kept them involved, giving them the fun they needed as a family. Angie might not have talked to her brother about their mother, but she'd never stopped looking up to him.

And now, she'd come to admire Laura.

"A penny for your thoughts? Unless you'd like some of this cotton candy." Laura's face was hidden behind the huge cone of pink spun sugar.

Jack laughed. "Psychologists charge a lot more than a penny. Not that I'm seeing one but maybe I should."

"Why?"

"My daughter just checked out Ben's roommate. Having a

college-aged son makes me feel old, but anticipating the next hour at this podunk fair makes me feel like a kid."

She grinned after swallowing a wad of fluff. "I'm glad you feel comfortable enough to share that."

"You've made me feel comfortable since I saw you mow your mother's lawn." Maybe he'd given too much away, but he felt like he'd known Laura longer than a few days.

"What's mowing the lawn got to do with it?"

Jack felt his face heat. "It's a guy thing."

Her eyebrows shot up. "You've really got to explain that one."

He ran his hand through his hair and glanced at Laura. She had a quirky tilt to her lips as if she'd heard every line a guy could throw. And no wonder. She looked sweeter than that candy.

"Well," he started, "guys find women doing so-called manly stuff attractive. At least I do."

"Mowing the lawn is manly?"

"If you get your hands dirty."

She gave him a who-are-you look.

He was making a muddle of this, but he couldn't control his words. They kept spilling out, like coffee grounds without a filter. "I'm all for soft and pretty, but when a woman participates in work that I enjoy, it's familiar for me. I don't have to try so hard to connect."

She giggled. He'd never expected to hear Laura Toivo giggle. "You don't like a Ms. Priss."

"It's way deeper than that." Whether he liked it or not, he'd already connected with Laura. Big time. It didn't mean he had to act on it. There was nothing he need do other than remain friends. And only friends.

"It's the same with women wanting a man who's sensitive, but not a wimp. Like a guy who not only mows his *own* lawn, but the old lady's next door."

"Exactly." She'd given herself away, too. And there was nothing light about the way she looked at him. He swallowed in an attempt to get rid of the cloying anticipation wracking his brain.

Laura focused on her cotton candy. Jack was no wimp. The strength she saw in him was incredibly attractive. He was the kind of man a woman could depend upon. He loved his kids. Even if he'd spent too much time building his practice like he said, Jack didn't strike her as the sort of dad who tried buying his way into his kids' hearts. He was too solid for that.

They passed rows of games and giant stuffed animals that only a child would love and Laura knew exactly how Jack felt about being a kid. She might as well be fifteen again. Her stomach pitched every time he leaned close to point out something new. She checked her watch. They had an hour before meeting Ben and Angie in front of the cotton-candy stand.

Jack pointed to the Ferris wheel. "Want to give it a try?"

Laura couldn't remember the last time she'd been on one. Anthony had always said they were stupid, and Brooke had been afraid of heights. She squared her shoulders. "We have to."

Jack bought tickets and then they waited in line.

When it was their turn to board, he offered his hand to help her climb into the cherry-colored car. She took it without hesitation. Climbing in took more grace than she possessed.

Sitting next to Jack, the attendant secured the safety bar. With a groan, the car swung upward only to lurch to a halt in order to load the next car.

Laura remembered the secret desire of every girl in high school. The summer was made complete by getting stuck at the top of the Ferris wheel with a cute boy.

Only Jack was no boy.

The space inside their little car seemed to shrink further. Laura gripped her cotton candy. As riders exited and new ones boarded, their car inched its way up and up.

"We're getting close to the top," Jack said.

Laura's mouth went dry. "Uh-huh."

"Wow! I can see for miles up here."

She watched him as he scanned the horizon. His profile was strong and rugged, and the corners of his eyes crinkled. Their car lurched upward again.

"What's that?" He pointed.

Laura focused on what lay in the distance. "That's Portage Lake. They have a nice beach if you want to take Angie."

He turned toward her. "Great idea."

She took a huge bite of her cotton candy. The piece she bit off was too big. Half of it stuck to the side of her mouth.

Jack laughed at her. "Nice."

Before Laura could respond, their car lurched to a stop.

At the top.

She held her breath when Jack leaned closer. She put her candy puff between them. "Here, you take a bite and see how well you do."

He looked surprised, amused even, but he did as ordered. His bite was also too big, draping spun sugar across his cheek to get stuck in his hair.

Laura automatically reached out and touched his face. She knew how sticky this stuff was in hair. If she could catch it before it melted…

She froze when Jack gently grabbed her wrist, keeping her hand in place. His gaze turned serious, his blue eyes dark and intent, like this morning when he'd bobbled the glass. Turning her palm, he nibbled the excess candy from her fingers.

Laura felt her mouth drop open. She searched for a smart remark but nothing came out.

"The second taste was sweeter."

Their car jerked to life and they spun backward fast. Laura wasn't prepared for the sudden movement. She fell into Jack's chest and nearly lost her puff over the back of their seat.

"Whoa." Jack steadied Laura's cotton candy cone with

one hand and wrapped his arm around her waist to keep her from sliding.

He didn't know what had come over him, but he certainly didn't mind the warmth of her plastered against him. By the loss of color in Laura's cheeks, he knew he'd shocked her. He'd shocked himself, too.

"Sorry." She straightened and slid to the far side of the seat. The cotton candy puff once again brandished between them like a shield.

"No problem."

The Ferris wheel jerked forward, gaining momentum.

Laura gripped the safety bar with one hand and her cotton candy with the other. She screeched as the ride sped up and her hair flew back and straight up. Her cheeks turned pink when she caught him staring. "What?"

"Nothing. Just enjoying the view." But he was trying to gain control over his inclination to pull her back into his arms.

She laughed and shook her head. Lightening the moment.

The ride finally slowed and repeated the process of switching passengers. Their car was next up to empty. It had been much too short a thrill, but Jack was glad just the same.

"Hey, Dad," Ben called.

Jack waved at his kids. Angie stood next to her brother with a giant stuffed animal. She looked puzzled.

Once they were back on solid ground, Angie ran toward them. "Look what Ben won."

He glanced at Laura. She wouldn't look at him. "Good job."

His son slapped him on the back, and whispered near his ear. "You are *so* busted."

"What?" But he knew exactly to what Ben referred. How long had his kids been waiting for them to end their Ferris wheel ride?

Ben gave him an insolent grin. "You know what. Nice moves."

Jack checked on his daughter pinching a wad from Laura's cotton candy. Had she seen them, too?

"Look, Ben…"

His son's eyebrows rose.

Jack realized he couldn't explain what had come over him. He'd acted on impulse. He'd just as soon blame the flirting on the spirit of a fun evening and leave it at that.

Ben grinned at him anyway. "I've got a ride back to campus, so I'm going to head out."

Jack pulled his son into a gruff hug. "Call my cell when you get into your dorm, I don't care how late it is."

"Aw, Dad."

"I mean it. Leave a message even if I'm asleep."

"Bye, Ben." Angie hugged the stuffed bear.

Jack glanced at Laura. She stood apart, watching them with a wistful smile curving her lips and holding that ridiculously large pink puff of spun sugar. He tried to imagine her suited up to meet with high-powered business owners. The deadly dealer of business solutions. She seemed too warm and caring for his first image of her. Laura Toivo wasn't a sales shark. She fit in with his family too well.

It was late by the time they got home. Laura slipped out of her convertible and yawned, her equilibrium finally returned. Her head had been spinning ever since she got on that Ferris wheel. Looking up into the moonless sky full of glittering stars, she was amazed at how dark the night was. Having Jack's SUV close behind had been comforting while driving the isolated country roads home.

"Come on, Ange, wake up." Jack roused his sleeping daughter.

"Need help?" Laura was ready to turn in, too.

"I got her. Do you mind if she stays one more night? We never got her things unpacked."

Laura opened the side door with her key. "Of course not. She's always welcome."

Jack got his daughter walking in the right direction, but

Angie mumbled and grumbled her way into the kitchen and headed straight upstairs.

"I'll make sure she finds the bed," he said.

Laura poured herself a glass of water from the kitchen sink and drained it with one long gulp.

"She's out cold," he said softly when he returned.

She flipped around. Her nerve endings tingled in her fingers and toes. "Would you like something to drink?"

"No, it's late."

Laura battled between disappointment and relief. "Thanks for a fun evening."

"Thanks for taking care of Angie today, and, uh—" Jack looked at the floor a moment before looking back at her. "I'm sorry if I made you uncomfortable."

She stared at him.

He stepped closer. "On the Ferris wheel."

Laura leaned farther against the sink, bracing for what might come. Could she duck this one? "No. Not at all, I mean, don't worry about it. Not a big deal."

He looked relieved.

But she was shaking in her shoes. If he tried to kiss her, she might let him. Not good. Not good at all. *Think of something else....*

"The leftovers!" She smacked her head with the palm of her hand. "I guess they're no good now, they've been in your truck all evening."

"I'll throw them away." Jack wore a lopsided grin. "You like a lot of junk food, don't you?"

Laura's breath hitched. "One of my many weaknesses."

"I don't know. You're pretty close to perfect, Laura Toivo."

No one had ever told her that. If she were a stick of butter, she'd slip right out of the wrapper. She'd just melted. "Thanks, Jack, but you don't know me very well."

He didn't speak. He didn't have to. He didn't look at her,

but through her. Right down to the depths of her heart as if looking for room and board there.

Not a chance. She'd posted a *No Trespassing* sign with every intention of keeping it firmly in place. Still, her vacant heart skipped a few beats. "Well, you do live next to my mother. I'm sure we'll see a lot of each other. Holidays and all that."

"We'll see." Jack had a way of making her wish for things.

"I think we're both tired and we should call it a night." She walked him to the door.

He stepped onto the porch and turned. Taking her hand in his, he lifted it to his lips for the lightest kiss. "Good night, Laura."

"Good night, Jack," she whispered, unable to breathe.

She leaned against the screen doorjamb because she couldn't remain standing without support. She watched him walk across the lawn and enter the barn before she finally turned out the light.

Laura sat up in bed and listened closely. She'd heard something. Nothing. She snuggled back under the covers and closed her eyes. A low moan made the hairs on the back of her neck stick out. She didn't move a muscle, only listened.

"Mom?" The voice was soft, young.

Laura's heart broke. She heard a groan of pain followed by a choking sound and Laura was out of bed and down the hall in a flash. Her heart thumping inside her chest, she knocked and then pushed opened the door. Angie sat in the middle of the full canopy bed with tears streaming down her face.

Was she awake or still in the grip of a dream? Laura sat on the edge of the bed. "Angie? What is it, what's wrong?"

Angie threw herself into Laura's arms and wailed, "I didn't mean to wake you up, but I…"

"Had a bad dream?" She felt Angie nod her head. She squeezed tighter. "Do you want to tell me about it?"

"It was Mom," she said with broken sobs. "She kept calling me, but I couldn't find her."

Laura felt the tension in Angie's back. She stroked her shoulders in an attempt to soothe her. "It's okay. It's okay to cry."

Angie crumpled into her, clinging. They stayed wrapped together for a long while before Angie's sobs subsided into hiccups.

Laura brushed the dark hair off Angie's forehead, unsure what else to do. "You okay?"

She tightened her hold. "Don't leave."

Laura reached for Angie's hand. It wouldn't be appropriate to stay with her in here, but she wouldn't leave her, either. "Come on, bring your pillow. We'll go downstairs and I'll make tea."

After dumping blankets and pillows in the living room, Laura put the teakettle on to boil. She arranged a sugar bowl and creamer next to one of her mother's teapots. Wondering if God was listening, she whispered a request, "Please, Lord, give me the right words."

Angie stood in the doorway, watching her movements. "When do you stop missing them?"

The kettle chugged and whined.

Angie looked fragile, a little girl lost without her mother and Laura's heart twisted. "You never stop missing them, but the hurt gets better with time."

"I miss Mom." Angie's voice was raw. "She would have liked tonight."

"I know."

"After she died, none of my friends had a clue what to say. I hated it that they still had a mom and I didn't. After a while, I stopped hanging out with them, except my friend Stacy. She never treated me any different." Angie looked at the stove.

"What about your brother?" Laura poured steaming water over tea bags.

Angie shrugged her shoulders. "He's always on Dad's side."

Laura cocked her head. "Your dad's side?"

Angie looked up with regret-filled eyes. "She didn't want to go. Mom told me she didn't want to go white-water rafting. She was only doing it for Dad. She made me promise not to tell him. But maybe if I did, they wouldn't have gone!" Angie burst into new tears.

Laura pulled her into her arms once again. "It's nobody's fault, Angie. Accidents happen. They're part of life."

"But why did God let it happen? He's supposed to protect people. I said my prayers at night to keep Mom and Dad safe but He didn't listen. Why, Laura? Why didn't God listen?"

Laura let out a sigh. "I don't know. I just don't know."

What could she say? She'd often wondered why God let bad things happen to good people. Still, she needed to ease this girl's guilt. Angie had no control over what her parents had decided to do. She had to show her that. But how?

Laura pulled back as an idea came to her. "Did your mom always do whatever your dad said?"

Angie looked confused. "No, but—"

"Give me an example that you remember."

Angie furrowed her brow. "Well, lots of times my mom wanted one thing and Dad another. Movies, furniture, food, stuff like that."

They were getting somewhere. Laura squelched the elation bubbling inside. This might make a difference. "Did your mom ever change his mind about that stuff, or get him to do what she wanted him to do after he said he wouldn't?"

Angie nodded.

"You see? Your mom made up her own mind to go on that rafting trip. She was doing something important by doing something for your dad."

"But Dad *made* her go."

"Do you really think so? It doesn't sound like your mom was someone easily persuaded. She may not have wanted to go, but love puts others first. Your mom knew it was important to your dad. She sounds like a very strong woman, Angie. I would have liked her."

Angie's eyes teared up again. But Laura knew she'd eased the pain a little. It hurt to think Angie had lost her faith and her willingness to believe in something larger than herself, larger than this life.

She cupped Angie's cheek. "My father used to say, regardless of what happens in life, God is still God."

"Do you believe in God?" Angie asked.

Laura didn't want Angie to lose faith. It would hurt Jack too much. Deep down, Laura wanted to believe. She wanted that rock-solid faith Jack had, but she didn't know how to get it. "I want to, Angie."

Chapter Nine

The loft needed finishing, and Jack needed Angie's help. He tapped again on the kitchen door of Laura's house. Were they both still asleep?

Again, no answer.

He tried the door and it opened to his touch. With a frown, he stepped inside, hoping everything was okay. The house was quiet. Dirty dishes lay in the sink along with a teapot, cups and an empty bag of store-bought cookies.

Laura and her snacks.

A sleepy-eyed vision of his thoughts wandered into the kitchen from the living room wearing a baggy T-shirt and pajama pants. Laura fished in the cupboard for a mug.

He watched her measure coffee grounds, pour water into the reservoir and flip the switch. Leaning against the counter, she looked at him as if seeing him in her kitchen was the most natural thing in the world.

"Morning," she said.

"Don't you lock your doors at night?"

She shrugged. "Usually, why?"

"I walked right in."

Her eyebrows lifted. "I must have left it open."

A surge of protectiveness engulfed him. He didn't like the idea of Laura and Angie in a big old house in the middle of nowhere with the door unlocked. "You need to be more careful."

She glared at him. "This isn't Lansing, Jack."

It didn't matter. He wanted her safe.

He noticed the dark smudges under her eyes. Something was wrong. "Is everything okay? You look like you had a rough night."

The coffeemaker hissed its last bit of water into the pot. Without answering Laura poured herself a cup. She cocked her head toward the living room. "Maybe it was the cotton candy."

"You sure it was just the candy?"

He'd thought about her last night and wondered if she'd gone through the same kind of torment. He liked how she made him feel young, as if his whole life still lay ahead. It was tempting to forget about her high-powered career in Wisconsin. He wouldn't.

Like most temptations, he'd skate close to the edge without falling through the ice.

But Laura Toivo was a temptation better left alone.

Besides, Angie came first. That meant getting plugged into a church with a good youth program, getting Angie settled into school. He had a vet practice to attend to, gradually taking over clients and building their trust. He couldn't relocate without making those connections within the community.

By the time Jack could even consider dating, Laura would be long gone.

She sipped her coffee. "Mmm, probably."

Jack peeked into the living room and spotted Angie under a blanket on the love seat. The couch also had a blanket and pillow. By the looks of it, they'd had a small pajama party with half-empty glasses of pop and an opened bag of chips left on the coffee table.

He frowned. "How'd you two end up down here?"

Laura looked in at Angie, as if making sure she was asleep. "We talked."

A sinking feeling laced through his gut. "You don't have to say a thing. I know what happened."

Laura remained silent.

Jack returned to the kitchen and helped himself to a cup of coffee. "I'm sorry she woke you. I thought Ange had these dreams licked, but maybe last night stirred up memories."

Laura's eyes widened. "She's had them before?"

"For a while, it was every night after Joanne's death. But Angie hasn't had one in over a year."

Laura stared into her coffee cup. "Did you seek help for her?"

Jack resumed his post against the counter. "I tried. Angie went to appointments with our church counselor, but she wouldn't open up. She wasn't ready to talk. Everyone I spoke with said this would resolve on its own. When the dreams stopped, I gave up trying to force the issue."

"Oh."

They both fell silent. He and his daughter had made serious headway since moving, but if the nightmares were back, he didn't want her to fall into old habits. "Maybe, I should have pushed harder for her to see a professional."

Laura stepped closer, concern in her eyes. "You did what you thought was best at the time."

"I believe Angie needs divine intervention. Her spirit was broken, and it's finally knitting itself back together. Only God can keep those stitches from unraveling. But she's got to let Him help her."

Laura looked thoughtful. "Anything I can do?"

"Keep doing what you're doing. Be her friend."

"And for you?"

Good question. Despite his worries for Angie, he wanted reassurance, comfort, something.

Laura wrapped her arms around his waist.

His hands slid around her back. How long had it been since he'd let himself need comforting? He'd kept a strong front for his kids. Through it all, God had been his life source, keeping him sane, keeping the guilt at bay. And he was grateful. But deep inside, something broke loose. He closed his eyes and pulled her closer.

Jack didn't want to hold on to Laura for too long, but he didn't want to let go, either.

She pulled back enough to search his eyes. "This can't be easy for you, either."

He touched her shoulders. "We shouldn't be doing this."

Her eyes widened. "It's just a hug."

"You know what I mean. The connection between us." Every reason to steer clear of Laura scattered when he looked into her eyes. She was good with Angie, and Ben liked her.

He felt her stiffen. "We'll just keep it simple and friendly. That's what we have to do."

Relieved that she understood, he nodded. "It's too complicated at this point."

She shrugged out of his arms and laughed. "With me, it's always complicated. Plus you have two kids. And I have a job I need to return to."

Angie stirred in the next room.

"Look, I've got to shower and get to the hospital. Mom's being released tomorrow."

"Thanks, Laura. For everything." The feelings running through him were anything but simple. Why'd God bring her into his life when a relationship wasn't right for either of them? But Angie needed Laura. The problem was that Jack was beginning to think he might need her, too.

With a sigh, Jack entered the living room and sat at the end of the loveseat. Angie was under there somewhere. He pulled the blanket back. She lay on her stomach, her face covered with a mass of tangled dark hair. He pushed it aside.

She grumbled.

"You awake?" he asked.

"I am now."

"How'd you and Laura end up down here?"

Only one eye looked at him and her body tensed. "What did she say?"

"Nothing much, only that you'd had too much cotton candy." He felt her shoulders give with relief. She wasn't going to tell him about her nightmare and that hurt.

He let out another weary sigh. "Ange, did you have one of your bad dreams?"

Her eye closed. "She told you, didn't she?"

"I'm not stupid. It's not like you haven't had these before. Remember that sleepover you went to? I got a call in the middle of the night."

"Laura didn't say anything?"

"She didn't have to." He touched her shoulder. "Want to talk about it?"

"Not really." She wouldn't look at him.

"Don't you think we should?"

She sat up straight, but her bottom lip trembled. Angie fought against the tears that looked ready to fall, but at least she wasn't shutting him out, turning away. Not yet anyway.

He stayed quiet, willing himself to stay put and listen if she opened up. In the past, he'd hurried the process, or backpedaled so he could duck and run. He'd never been ready to hear what was on his daughter's mind. He didn't want to hear the words he carried around come out of her mouth.

It's your fault.

Angie wound the blanket around her like a shield.

He couldn't take the pained expression on her face, so he pulled her to his chest. Coward that he was, he took the easy way out. "It's okay, sweetheart. We can talk about it another time."

She wilted against him. "Thanks, Dad."

He held her tight. They were making progress. Angie wasn't pulling away from him. She accepted his comfort and that small victory made his heart sing.

When he finally let her go, they both laughed as they wiped their wet cheeks. Slapping his knees, he asked, "How about spending the afternoon at the beach? We'll call Ben and see if he can join us."

Angie's eyes lit up. "Can we go now?"

"First breakfast, and then your loft."

"Laura said I could make pancakes this morning."

"She did, huh?"

"Come on, Dad. I might even flip a few."

"Morning, Mom." Laura entered her mother's hospital room with a couple of shopping bags.

Her mom scoped out the bags with a lift of an eyebrow. "Where've you been?"

"I had to pick up a bathing suit since the Stahls invited me to the beach. I found a couple of outfits for you. Something cool to wear home. It's supposed to be hot the rest of the week."

Her mother was not as thin as she used to be but she'd never be considered heavy. Even so, she wore dresses nearly every day complete with hose, girdle and slip. She'd roast.

"I have plenty of clothes."

"Not like these." Laura pulled out three different capri pants sets in light summer fabrics: seersucker, cotton jersey knit and gauze.

Her mom discarded her booklet of crossword puzzles and caressed the material. "These must have cost you a fortune."

That was as good a statement of gratitude as Laura could expect. "They were on sale."

"Where's your swimsuit?"

Laura rustled through tissue paper and pulled out a hot-pink tankini. "What do you think?"

"I think that young man will enjoy the view."

"What?"

"Angie's dad."

"Mom!" Laura felt her face flame. "What makes you think he'd even look?"

She countered with a coy smirk that said she wasn't born yesterday. "Aunt Nelda's been filling me in."

"On what? There's nothing to tell." Laura waved her hand in dismissal. But that wasn't quite true. She and Jack danced around their attraction, even though they both knew it couldn't go anywhere.

"Nancy saw you at the fair last night."

News traveled the express route in the Toivo family. "Why didn't Nancy talk to me?"

"You were on the Ferris wheel and her boy was sick." Her mother's gaze narrowed. "Does he stay in the house *with* you?"

Laura bristled. "No, Mom. No. Jack's in the apartment. Angie's been in my old room only until her bedroom in the loft is finished from installing a window."

"Well, you better be careful. I don't want to hate my neighbor."

"Why on earth would you do that? You've met Jack's daughter. He's just as nice."

"If you two broke up, I'd have to choose sides."

"We aren't a couple, Mom. It's impossible. He's got two teenagers he's focused on and I have my career."

Still, she was heading for the beach after leaving the hospital. But she'd brought her laptop so she could work through the afternoon there. It was too hot to do anything but lounge lakeside.

Her mom pursed her lips. "After you broke up with Anthony, you only came home for Christmas. You hardly come home as it is. If it's bad between you and Jack, you won't *ever* come home."

Laura bit back a defensive retort. Her mom was right. She'd brought Anthony home only once. He'd criticized the area and that had raised her mother's hackles. Not a fun visit. "Work is busy."

Her mother's eyes softened. "Maybe you're too busy, Laura. Life has a way of passing a person by if they don't slow down enough to enjoy it."

Laura grit her teeth. If she got that promotion, her free time would be even less. She'd have to travel more. But something worth having didn't come without a sacrifice. She knew that. "I'll do better."

The doctor entered and checked her mother's charts. They discussed meds and changes in her mother's diet as well as home health aides. Laura jotted down the name of the nurse in charge of the home health care programs managed by their senior center.

After the doctor left, Laura grabbed one of her mother's crossword puzzle books. Maybe she should skip the beach.

Her mom looked surprised. "Aren't you going to be late?"

"For what?"

"Putting that pink swimsuit to use."

Laura smiled. "I don't know. Maybe I want to hang out here instead. It's cooler."

Her mother gave her a look like she couldn't be fooled. "It's too pretty outside to stay indoors. Tomorrow, you'll be waiting on me hand over foot."

Well, well, well. Laura was floored. No martyr today. "Are you trying to get rid of me?"

Her mother laughed. "Yes, I am. Please, go have fun while you can."

Laura leaned down and kissed her mother's cheek. "I guess I'll see you tomorrow, then."

Her mom smiled. "Tomorrow."

Laura searched the packed beach for Jack. She'd called from the hospital parking lot, and he'd given her an idea of where they'd set up their green-and-white striped umbrella. He'd said they were left of the concession stand.

She easily spotted Jack's broad shoulders. His arms were well defined. The rest of him wasn't bad, either.

Sluicing through the sand, Laura dropped her bag by their blanket.

Angie perused a fashion magazine, but quickly tossed it aside. "Hey, Laura, Dad's got a question for you."

Laura raised an eyebrow toward Jack.

"Give her a chance to relax a minute, will you?" Jack said.

"It's okay. I can't stay too long. Mom's coming home tomorrow and I want to move her room downstairs tonight. So, what's the question?" Laura arranged her towel next to their blanket.

"We stopped by the school so Angie could get a look around. We picked up the eighth-grade syllabus and Ange is going to need a computer. Ben took our old PC to college along with his laptop. We were wondering if you could give us a few pointers on what to buy."

Laura smiled at his daughter's excitement. "Laptop or desktop?"

Jack and Angie answered at the same time with different preferences. For obvious reasons, Ange wanted a laptop. They looked cool.

Laura laughed. "I'd be happy to help. There's an electronics store here in Houghton. We could check that out."

"In exchange for helping us choose a computer, we'll help with your mom's room if you stay. Deal?" Jack asked.

She shielded her eyes from the sun as she looked up at him. "That might work."

"You know it will." He sat down on the blanket next to Angie who shoved potato chips into her mouth while her toes dug in the sand.

Laura unpacked her laptop and settled onto her towel, ready to get some work done. "How's the water?"

"Ange is too chicken to go in."

"It's cold," Angie whined.

"Youth is wasted on the young," Jack said. "Come on, Ange. It's too hot to just lay here."

"I just put on sunscreen."

"You can put more on later." He threw a handful of sand on his daughter.

"Cut it out."

He did it again.

Laura laughed as Angie jumped up, hands on hips, obviously thinking what she might do to retaliate. She didn't have time. Jack flung his daughter over his shoulder and headed for the shore.

Angie screeched the whole way.

She watched father and daughter splashing until they were knee-deep. Ben arrived with two friends in tow. They said a quick hello then ran toward the water, T-shirts flying, to join in the fun. The whole lot of them headed for deeper water.

Laura launched into some work on her laptop. After an hour, her concentration was shot. Her attention dragged toward the water every time she heard Jack laugh.

There was something about being at the beach that made a person feel like they didn't have a care in the world. This was what life was about. Real connections, real relationships. Not substituting superficial sales calls for human interaction.

Her heart skipped a beat. She'd miss this. She'd miss them.

Her mom's warning took on new meaning.

Be careful....

Chapter Ten

Laura checked her watch. It was past time she got home and moved her mother's room downstairs. After the beach, Laura helped Jack and Angie at the computer store. A complete personal computer, laser printer and compatible laptop later, the three of them stopped for a bite to eat. Laura promised she'd set up the computer, feeling like she'd led Jack to spend more than he'd planned.

In the parking lot, Jack yawned. "I've got to hit the grocery store, but then we'll be over to help with moving your mother's room."

Angie slumped her shoulders. "I don't want to go to the store. Can I ride home with Laura?"

"If it's okay with Laura." Jack looked at her. "Do you need anything?"

"Nope. Angie can come with me."

Summer days made Laura grateful for her convertible. The hot afternoon had mellowed with a gentle breeze. The country-side had taken on a golden haze and everything slowed to nearly a stop. Except her. Her mind raced with what she needed to do before she could call it a night. She checked her rearview mirror and then passed a truck pulling an overloaded hay wagon.

She glanced at Angie sitting in the passenger seat, her dark hair blowing in the wind. Long strands whisked across her face. "Did you have a chance to talk to your dad about your dream last night?"

Angie shook her head. "I couldn't do it."

Laura concentrated on the road. She wanted to do this for Jack. Try to make things better somehow. "It was a horrible accident. No more your dad's fault than yours."

"I know." Angie smiled as she held her hair back.

Laura smiled, too. "He needs to hear that, especially coming from you."

"I know." But Angie sighed, before adding quietly, "Thanks."

Laura's throat tightened. "For what?"

"For getting it."

"Yeah, I get it." As she pulled in the drive, speech wasn't an option. Like watching a touching movie and trying not to cry, Laura struggled for composure.

"Want to see my room? It came out pretty cool." Hauling her beach bag, Angie fished her key out of her tiny purse.

Grateful for the change of subject, Laura said with vigor, "Absolutely."

Jack kept the place tidy. His bed was made and the dishes were washed and neatly stacked. She followed Angie up the spiral staircase to the small loft. With colorful window treatments, bunk beds covered with bright quilts and the splashy new purple rug on the floor, Angie's room looked young and fresh.

"This is perfect."

Angie smiled. "Do you like it?"

Laura peeked through the curtain of hanging plastic beads into a custom-made closet. Jack had done impressive work, maximizing the small space. "I love it."

A picture of a woman with dark hair like Angie's caught Laura's attention. She picked up the frame. "Is this your mom?"

Angie nodded.

"She's lovely."

"So are you," Angie said.

An odd comment. Laura wasn't trying to compete with Jack's late wife. Did Angie think she was? She carefully replaced the photo. "It's important to honor your mom by keeping her memory alive."

"I finally put her picture out."

Laura could have cried. "Keep it out, Angie, forever."

"I will."

It was getting late and Laura had a lot to do. "I better start on my mother's room. Tell your dad that he can pop over whenever, and you, too, if you want to but it's not a big deal if you don't."

"I'm going to change first, I have sand in my bathing suit."

Laura laughed and made her way out of Jack's apartment. Once inside her mother's house, Laura also changed into shorts and a T-shirt, and then charged downstairs. She'd tackle cleaning the spare room until Jack came over to help her move the big stuff from upstairs.

Boxes of pictures and Christmas decorations lined the hallway. Laura brushed the sweat from her brow when she heard Jack's footsteps in the kitchen. She came around the corner and noticed that he looked sunburned. Bronzed was a better word. Golden. He still wore his navy swim trunks, flip-flops and a gray T-shirt. He carried plastic bags in each hand.

"What's all that?"

"Replacements for the pancakes this morning."

"You didn't have to do that."

He smiled. "I wanted to."

Laura didn't bother putting the dry goods away. She could take care of that after Jack left. It took a couple hours to haul her mother's furniture downstairs, arrange and then rearrange it the way Laura wanted it. Jack had been a trooper. Angie had bailed before they'd finished. The kid couldn't keep her eyes open. She curled up on the couch under a cotton afghan crocheted by Aunt Nelda.

That left Laura alone with Jack. His presence overwhelmed the room. Laura grew fidgety—moving her mother's doilies around only to finally remove them.

"You're awfully quiet," Jack said.

"I've never had to take care of anyone before. I don't want to botch it." Laura stood next to Jack as they surveyed their handiwork. Finished at last.

Jack folded his arms. He smelled like fresh air and the lake and something less defined but very male. "Just relax. You'll do great. I'm sure your mom will appreciate this."

"You don't know my mother."

"She can't be that bad. She raised you." Jack faced her.

Laura turned, too. "I drove her nuts the whole time. I don't think my mother wanted to have kids, but I showed up anyway, uninvited. Sometimes, I think she'd have been happier without me."

Jack gave her a lopsided grin. "I don't believe that."

"Like I said before, you don't know me well."

"I know that you care for my daughter, that you're a woman of integrity and you love your mom no matter how much you complain about her." His eyes held a challenge to dispute those facts.

She couldn't. She didn't want to. But she needed to get them out of this bedroom. "How about something to drink?"

"That'd be great." He followed her into the kitchen.

She poured lemonade, glad for something else to do. "Thank you for helping. I couldn't have done this without you."

He drained his glass, set it on the counter, and stepped toward her. "It's the least I can do."

She couldn't look away from him. She couldn't, move either. The pull between them intensified, or maybe that was her heart beating loud enough to ring in her ears and make her dizzy.

"Jack—"

He caressed her cheek. "I better go."

"Sure." Her voice came out with a strangled sound of relief. "I'll get Angie."

Laura leaned against the sink in the kitchen. It made her smile to overhear Jack rouse his sleeping daughter. His gentle teasing, and Angie's grumbles. They'd brought life back into this house.

Angie scuffled through the kitchen and headed for the porch. "Night, Laura."

"Good night, Angie."

Laura watched Jack and Angie walk across the yard before she shut the door. She cared about them. Maybe, too much. Fear coiled in her gut. What did she think she was doing? She couldn't take another blow to her heart, could she?

Jack looked up at the dusky-blue sky scattered with glimmers of light and wished for what he knew wasn't right. Torn by the unwise idea to march back to Laura's and kiss her, Jack rubbed his forehead. But he kept walking. Following his daughter to their apartment.

This was crazy. They'd moved in a little over a week ago. He said he'd never again rush things in life, but here he was caring for Laura. It was too soon. Much too soon.

Angie had left the door to the barn opened and she'd forgotten to leave on a light. Stumbling over discarded strips of wood, he banged his knee against his gas grill. Sucking in a gulp of air, he let loose a groan of frustration.

And then he heard a whimper.

Feeling along the wall, he found the light switch and flipped it on. In the corner, huddled against his plastic wrapped sectional couch, was a scruffy pooch with matted hair. It was all black with big brown eyes on either side of a huge black nose. It looked like a cross between a poodle and a Schnauzer—pathetically cute.

"What is it, Dad?" Angie asked with a sleepy voice.

Jack squatted down, holding out his hand. "A dog. Come here, fella."

The dog whined again and shivered.

"Oh, can we keep him?"

"Stay back a minute, Ange." Jack leaned forward, his palm open to the mutt. He wanted to be sure it was safe, before he let his daughter hold him.

The dog decided to trust him. With a submissive crawl, the little guy inched forward until he was close enough to lick Jack's fingers.

"Come on," he said.

Once the dog got close enough, Jack carefully picked him up. A male. Jack guessed he was not yet a year old. The little guy's bones were easily felt through his wiry coat and he didn't have a collar.

Angie opened the door to their apartment.

"Get him a bowl of water," Jack said.

Angie set the dish on the floor, and then they watched the dog lap it up like he hadn't had any in days.

Jack ruffled the dog's fur. "Where've you been, big guy? What happened to you?"

He'd often heard how folks up north didn't think twice about dumping dogs off on country roads or near farms. It never ceased to set his teeth to clench. By the looks of it, this little dog had been wandering awhile.

The dog sat down and looked at him expectantly.

"Now what?" Angie asked.

"Now food. Ange, tear up some bread and soak it with milk." Bland was the way to go. He didn't know when the dog had last eaten.

He watched the scrappy fellow scarf down the bread. Jack hoped this little dog didn't belong to anyone. Angie already loved him. So did he.

* * *

The next morning, Jack scraped breakfast leftovers into a plastic bowl for the dog.

"Come on, Dad, please? Can we keep him?" Angie asked.

"Depends on if anyone claims him. I'm going to take him to Dr. Walter's office and see if he knows anything."

"But you said he was a stray." Angie sat on the floor and rolled a tennis ball for the dog.

"Probably."

"So nobody wants him."

He laughed. Angie had always wanted a dog. She wasn't about to give this one up. Hopefully they didn't have to. "What should we call him?"

Angie shrugged.

"He's got to have a name." Jack set the plastic bowl on the floor. That brought the dog running.

Angie sat with a bounce on Jack's bed. She picked up the framed photograph of Joanne from his bedside table. She ran her fingers across the glass. "Do you still love Mom?"

Jack looked at his daughter closely. What had spurred that question? "I loved your mother very much and nothing will change that. I'll never forget her, Ange."

His daughter nodded, but she looked troubled, like she needed to talk. He grabbed a chair from the kitchen table and brought it close to his bed. Sitting down, he met her gaze. "What's on your mind?"

"Laura said it would be better if I told you, that maybe it would help."

He held his breath. "What's that?"

Angie's eyes welled with tears. "I miss her. I miss Mom."

Jack shifted to the bed and gathered Angie in his arms. He kissed the top of her head. "I know, honey. I do, too. I wish I'd never taken her to Colorado."

Angie rested her head on his shoulder. "You didn't know." Her voice was tight, choked. "I should have told you she didn't want to go, but Mom made me promise not to."

Jack nearly groaned. Angie had kept her promise bound up inside all this time, as if it might have made a difference if she'd tattled. Why would Joanne ask her not to tell? Why put that on a kid?

He cupped Angie's chin and tipped her head up so he could look at her. "I did know, Angie. I knew Mom didn't want to go. I lived with her long enough to know when she didn't want to do something even if she never said a word. But I ignored her concerns, her fear of water."

His tongue grew thick, his throat dry. He felt sick reliving his regrets. The guilt. "I cast them aside because I thought she was being silly."

Her eyes widened.

He forced the words out. "We went because of me, Ange. She wanted to make me happy. I'm to blame, not you."

Her hand found his and she squeezed it tight. "It's okay, Dad. Accidents are part of life."

Jack felt a tear run down his cheek. This new grown-up approach of hers hurt and soothed at the same time. Another tear fell and he swallowed hard. "I love you, Ange. You know that, don't you?"

She nodded.

He pulled her in for a bear hug and didn't let go. "We're going to get through this. Mom would want us to remember the good things we had, the good times. She'd want us to keep having them, too, Ange. She wouldn't want us to stop just because she's no longer with us."

They were going to make it. Moving up here had been the right decision, and Laura had been the sounding board his daughter needed to release her guilt, and the promise she'd made to her mother. He'd never expected to find so much in such a short amount of time. But after he'd released control to God, things had a way of coming together.

The dog jumped up on the bed and pushed his way under their arms, wiggling into the embrace.

Angie giggled. "His hair is so wiry."

"He's a hairy one." Jack petted the dog.

"Let's call him Harry."

Jack glanced at Angie and gave her another squeeze. "It fits. Come on, if we're going to make it to church, we better get moving."

After getting dressed, Jack stepped outside with Harry for a last-minute potty run before they left. He saw Laura, cell phone to her ear, walking toward her car. He could tell she was talking about her work. She tended to rest her hand on her hip when she spoke to whomever it was that covered for her. Her face looked grim when she hung up.

"What's up?" He walked toward her.

She smiled. "You look nice."

He'd ironed a pair of khaki's and a short-sleeved polo shirt. "You look worried."

She spotted Harry. "It's work. Hey, where'd he come from?"

"He snuck into the barn last night. I hope he's a stray. We're calling him Harry."

Laura bent down to nuzzle the dog. "He's adorable. Are you going to keep him?"

"If no one claims him. Is everything okay with work?"

She straightened with a sigh. "A prospective client wants more quotes on services. My manager won't let my assistant give them. They have to come from me, or the client will get reassigned to another salesperson."

"That's not good?"

"It makes Cindy, my assistant, feel helpless."

"But you're on family leave. Surely they'll cover for you."

"Existing clients, yes, but potential sales are different. I've spent months cultivating leads, calling on owners and tech managers. There's only so long they can wait before going elsewhere. I'll call the company tomorrow and see what I can do."

He didn't understand her world. Vets covered for each other all the time. They shared clients, customers, whatever. "Sounds like a tough line of work. Are you commissioned?"

Her eyes widened and he realized too late that he'd asked too personal a question.

She shrugged. "Salary plus commission."

"Well, there you go. You're still getting paid."

She gave him a crooked smile that clearly said he didn't have a clue, but thanks for trying. "I'm on my way to pick up my mom. Her tests were canceled, so she's ready now. I better go."

She looked frazzled. Anxious.

"If you can handle cutthroat sales, you can handle your mother."

She laughed then. "You've never met her."

"I'm looking forward to it. Call my cell if you need me."

He watched Laura slide behind the wheel of her powder-blue convertible. The urge to protect her from ever feeling anxious again ripped through. Who was he to think he could shelter Laura from worry. Jack definitely needed to put some space between them and fast. Good thing he'd start working with Dr. Walters, and Laura was bound to be busy with her mother. Once their daily routines kicked in, these feelings between him and Laura would surely fade.

Chapter Eleven

"Whose truck?" Laura's mom pointed to Jack's SUV as they pulled in the driveway.

"It belongs to the guy who bought the barn." Laura jumped out of her car and offered her mother a hand, ignoring how her damp cotton shirt stuck to her back.

Laura had put her convertible top up in order to run the air-conditioner, but her mother complained it was too cold so they resorted to opened windows that blew in hot air.

"Need a hand?" Jack, still dressed in his church clothes, walked toward them.

Angie trotted along, too.

"Mom, this is Jack Stahl, Angie's dad. This is my mother, Anna Toivo."

Jack extended his hand. "Nice to finally meet you, Mrs. T."

The dog slipped out of the barn door with a yip and dashed their way, diverting her mother's attention.

"Laura, please don't tell me you got a dog." Her mom's tone was stern, disapproving.

Jack let his hand drop. "His name is Harry. He wandered into the barn last night."

Her mom gestured for the dog to shoo. "Well, he can just wander back wherever he came from."

"Mom, Harry's their dog, not ours." Laura looked at Jack. Thank goodness he didn't offend easily.

With an indulgent smile, Jack reached into the backseat and hoisted her mother's suitcase high. He followed them into to the house. "He's a good dog, Mrs. T., and smart, too. My daughter loves him to pieces. We'll do our best to keep him out of your way."

"Harrumph." Her mother leaned against Laura.

Angie scooped up the dog before he got underfoot. "Sorry. Hi, Mrs. Toivo."

Her mom mumbled something that sounded like hello, but Laura couldn't be sure.

Laura reminded herself that her mom had been up since dawn, prepped, and then left in a hallway for tests that were eventually canceled. She braced herself for her mother's criticism as she led her into the relocated bedroom.

"Oh, Laura, what did you do?"

Jack took the wind out of her mother's complaint ready to set sail. He marched past them and dropped the suitcase on the bed. "Laura worked hard to make your room perfect. She figured the ground floor would give you time to get your strength back. It's a great idea."

Then he grinned as if daring her mother to complain.

She didn't. "It'll do for now."

Laura glanced at Jack and mouthed the words *thank you.* "Come on, Mom. Let's check out that shower seat I bought at the hospital and then you can take a nap."

"Lunch, then a nap." Her mother's tone sounded sharp, but then she smiled. "It's good to be home."

Monday morning, Jack scooped up Harry and headed into town and Dr. Joe Walter's office. Entering the older vet's examining room, Jack might as well have stepped back in time. Joe Walter fulfilled every expectation of a country vet. No computers, no high-tech equipment, just simple animal care given with years of experience. Jack looked forward to taking over the practice and implementing updated services, but he planned to keep the hands-on, personal touch.

But the bifocal wearing Joe Walter had scrawled his accounts into ledger books. Jack wasn't about to keep that up. He'd have to get the information into a computer somehow. Good thing he'd listened to Laura and purchased both a regular PC and a laptop. He wouldn't have to fight Angie in the evenings. They could both get their work done.

"Hey, Jack, what'cha got there?"

Jack hoisted the dog onto the examining table. "This is Harry. Have you seen him before? Or heard about a lost dog fitting this description?"

Dr. Walter peered over his bifocals. "Can't say that I have. He was probably dumped."

"That's what I thought when he wandered into my barn," Jack said. Harry was most likely a stray, and that bode well for keeping him.

"Might as well give him his shots."

Jack rubbed Harry's neck when the pooch trembled. "It's okay, fella."

Dr. Walter laid out a distemper shot and rabies booster. "I'm glad you came by this morning, I have some appointments I could use your help with if you're available for a few hours."

Jack would let Angie know not to expect him home until well after lunch. "Mind if Harry hangs out?"

"What's a vet's office without a dog? That's Buddy." The old man gestured to an ancient golden retriever that lounged on a dog bed.

"Exactly." Jack watched Harry closely as the dogs sniffed one another. No problems there.

"So, are you and your daughter settled in?"

"Pretty much. We bought Anna Toivo's barn and twenty acres. It'll be the perfect place for this practice."

Dr. Walter looked thoughtful. "I knew Anna's husband. Good man, God rest his soul. They had a daughter, but I can't say I've seen her lately. I don't think she lives here."

An image of what could be if Laura stayed in the area assaulted Jack. He didn't go there. "She lives in Wisconsin, but she's back home until Anna recovers from a stroke."

Dr. Joe Walter shook his balding head with disgust. Whether from the news of Anna's misfortune, or that her daughter didn't live nearby, Jack wasn't sure. "Come on, I'll show you the file on the dog that's coming in. I think he's terminal."

Those were the tough ones, knowing no matter what you did the dog was going to die. Jack had often wrestled with prolonging the inevitable. In the end, he liked to think he did what was best for the animal, whether he alleviated or ended their suffering. But sometimes, the owners insisted on every available treatment regardless of the trauma the dog endured. He hoped this wasn't one of those times.

It was late afternoon by the time Jack got home. He'd checked on Angie every couple of hours by cell phone. He knew his daughter was old enough to stay home alone for a good part of the workday, but he took comfort knowing Laura was next door if Angie needed anything.

He slipped into the apartment and Harry ran straight for Angie. "Hi, honey. How'd it go today?"

"Laura set up our computer."

Laura looked up at him, her gaze intent. "Let me know if you want the monitor positioned differently, or the tower."

He hadn't realized she was seated in his big office chair. Laura looked like she belonged there, with Angie. It was a nice scene to come home to. "I'm sure it's fine."

Laura quickly looked away and stood. "Well, I'd better get back. My mom's probably awake from her nap."

"Laura said she'd show me how to make a spreadsheet and give me tips on writing papers and junk." Angie tossed a squeaky toy to Harry.

"Maybe Laura can clue me into the best way to handle these." Jack tumbled a stack of ledgers onto the desk.

She ran her fingers across the worn leather covers, then flipped through the pages. "What are they? Inventories? Receivables?"

"Dr. Walter is a paper sort of guy. In a nutshell, *these* are the practice. Clients, their pets, their outstanding charges, payments made to date. You name it."

Laura's eyes widened. "You're kidding me. All by hand?"

Jack laughed. "He's old-fashioned."

"He's crazy. Doesn't he have someone do his books?"

"He's got an accountant that I met with to make sure the practice was sound. Looks like I need to get computerized and quick."

Laura gave him a smile that he sensed won over many a prospective client. "I know just the program you need."

"I knew you would."

For two days, between seeing to her mother's needs, and keeping tabs on her job, Laura spent an hour with Angie on the computer and then another hour or two with Jack after he came home from work. She'd set him up with a simple business program and showed him how to input the data, create bills, reconcile accounts and keep track of inventories.

"How can I input pet files to keep track of medical records."

Laura stepped back from peering over his shoulder. The subtle scent of his cologne teased her nose. "We could create a spreadsheet or a notes chart. What would really work for you is a tablet PC."

Jack gave her a look of complete ignorance.

"You can write on the screen like a pad of paper, but it's a laptop and the information will be saved."

Jack shook his head. "You know a lot about computers for a salesperson."

"I used to be a computer programmer. I moved up to tech staff, then finally to sales."

"Impressive."

Laura gobbled up the praise she read in his eyes. "Thanks."

"What's your favorite job so far?"

"The one I'm trying to get. A promotion to senior sales executive."

"More of the same?"

"Bigger. Larger clients, more territory, bigger commissions. You name it. Although, I did enjoy working on accounts with the tech staff and being part of making a business grow."

Jack's eyes narrowed.

"What?"

"Nothing. It's satisfying, being part of something you helped create."

Laura shrugged. She'd never really thought of it that way. She'd been in a support role, part of a team. "I guess. Well, I better head back. You guys have done a great job with this apartment. It looks nice."

"Next projects are fixing the pasture fence and adding a laundry hookup."

"If you need to use my mom's, it's not a problem." Laura glanced at Angie who was sprawled across her father's bed with her nose glued to the laptop.

Jack shrugged. "No use letting my washer and dryer collect dust. How's Anna feeling?"

"Today? She got angry with the physical therapist. They might have pushed her too hard, but it's for her own good. She needs to build her strength. She's a little cranky today."

Her mother was the most stubborn person Laura knew. She

wouldn't admit to loving Jack and Angie as neighbors, even though her mother looked forward to having Angie over for lunch, and last night Jack and Angie had joined them for dinner. It was nice, but weird, like they were forging a family.

Jack washed his hands at the kitchen sink. "Who isn't, from time to time?"

When he turned around, Laura sat on the braided area rug rolling a ball to Harry. The dog brought it back and dropped it into her lap. She looked cool in a sleeveless white cotton top and khaki shorts. Her hair had been whisked into a tiny pony-tail that stuck straight out. Wisps of her fine hair fell against her neck.

He appreciated the time she'd spent with them going over the computer. She was a patient teacher, and the depth of her knowledge about running a business had surprised him. She'd be fantastic managing an office. His office.

"He's adorable," Laura said.

"Yeah." He didn't give a hoot about the dog.

"Are there any cookies left?" Angie snapped her laptop closed.

Jacks thoughts halted. He'd forgotten his daughter was in the room. "There should be, unless you ate them all."

Angie slid off the bed and pulled out a bag of Oreos from the cupboard. "Want some cookies, Laura?"

Laura perked up. "Those are my favorite."

Jack laughed. "Nothing's better than homemade chocolate chip. Store-bought cookies *cannot* be your favorite."

Laura stared at him as if he were crazy. "Why not?"

"'Cause they're junk."

"That's what makes them so good."

"See, Dad. I told you," Angie chimed in.

He'd bought them for Angie who'd given him the same lame reason.

Laura ruffled Harry's head as she stood up. She washed her

hands before slipping into a chair at their table. "Just a couple, then I really have to go."

Jack poured milk for all of them. "Thursday, we're heading to my sister's in Lansing for the Labor Day weekend. We're taking Harry with us so he won't be in your way."

Laura smiled, her lips dotted with black cookie crumbs. "He's not in anyone's way. I think my mom's developed a soft spot for him. She calls him her little man."

Jack caught the exchanged glances between Angie and Laura. Obviously, Harry'd been to Anna's house. And so had Angie, every day for lunch. It eased his mind knowing that his daughter wasn't bored stuck at home. Next week school started, and Angie would no doubt make friends when the whirlwind of school activities would kick in. He was grateful to Laura and her mom for making his daughter's last days of summer count with berry picking, walking Harry and prepping for school by learning a new computer.

"Thanks for the cookies." Laura got up from the table.

He walked her to his door, his thoughts swirling with possibilities. There was Angie to consider. Ben, he knew would be fine. But the distance… Laura's place was six hours away. Could they adjust to seeing each other only on weekends when she came home? Would she even want to?

Later that night, Jack stumbled through his door to let Harry out. Clouds played peekaboo with a quarter moon and the warm air felt heavy. He saw the shadow of someone sitting on the porch swing, and before he could stop the dog, Harry took off toward the house.

"Great." He ducked back into his apartment, grabbed a T-shirt and slouched into it. By the time he'd made it to the porch, Harry lay curled in Laura's lap.

"I was about to bring him to you, but I had to give him one more snuggle."

Jack envied the dog. "He's got everyone wrapped around his paw."

"No one's asked about him, have they?" Laura said.

"Not a soul. I think it's safe to claim him."

Laura nodded.

"You're up late." Jack leaned against a porch post.

"I couldn't sleep."

He could feel the tension in her. After a stretch of silence, he asked. "You want to talk about it?"

She sighed. "My mother tries my patience."

He noticed the subtle jabs Anna had thrown at Laura during dinner last night. Things like she worked too hard, or her eyes would cross staring at that laptop. Silly comments, but he could tell they bothered Laura. "What's that all about?"

Laura shrugged. "I feel like I'm in her way, and then I feel guilty for not being around. It's a catch-22."

"Hmm."

"We've been carrying on this way all my life. I'm used to it. But with this stroke…"

"What?"

She shook her head. "I'm responsible for her, but I want my own life, too. I want that promotion."

"There's always options, Laura." He didn't like seeing her stressed. Jack noticed how Laura's shoulders stiffened when she got a call from her work. And ever since Anna had come home from the hospital, Laura had grown edgier, impatient. She talked about the promotion more, too.

She grinned then. "They're called home health aides, and I can't wait to get one hired."

Which meant she'd leave. Where would that leave Angie? And him?

Jack caught a flash of heat lightning out of the corner of his eye. It illuminated the clouds with pink and blue light. "Did you see that?"

Laura scooted over, Harry still in her lap. "Have a seat and watch."

He accepted her invitation with a slight creak from the swing.

"Are you ready for your trip?" Laura stroked Harry's fur.

"I'm not thrilled about the drive, but Angie's looking forward to it."

"She's a sweet girl. She showed me a picture of her mom. Were you and Joanne high school sweethearts?" Laura said.

"No." Jack clasped his hands in his lap and leaned back against the swing. "She was the new girl our senior year. Her dad was a minister assigned to a congregation in Okemos. I gave her a ride home a few times after football practice. She was a cheerleader but definitely a do-not-touch kind of girl."

Laura raised her eyebrow, but nodded for him to go on.

Jack cleared his throat. He'd only told his son this story as a warning. What would Laura think of him when she heard it? "Our senior trip was to Myrtle Beach. There were beach parties and Joanne and I hooked up. One thing led to another and one month after graduation we were married with Ben on the way."

Laura's eyebrows rose. He'd surprised her yet again.

Jack straightened. "As a kid, I didn't care much about consequences."

Her eyes narrowed. "Yet, you made it to college."

"Part of the marriage deal. Dad gave me a choice, marry Joanne or pay for college myself."

"That's a bit harsh, don't you think?" She looked as if he'd sacrificed too much.

He hadn't sacrificed enough. "I owed it to Ben to be there when he grew up, to provide a stable home."

"Still, I'm impressed that you and Joanne stayed together."

"We almost didn't. I was a freshman in college and married with a baby on the way. I resented it. If it wasn't for God revealing Himself, we might have ended in divorce."

Laura tipped her head. "How do you mean?"

"Joanne was raised in a Christian family She knew who to turn to in times of trouble. I didn't. I left her alone a lot. I was angry, confused, you name it. She prayed for me to wake up and realize what I had—a wife who wanted to make things work. Seeing Ben born was the miracle I needed to change. I chose to love their mother for better or worse and I decided right then that I wanted God in my life."

Laura chewed her bottom lip. "How'd you do that?"

He knew she was searching. There was an empty restlessness in her that she tried to fill with work. It wouldn't work. He'd been there. "I chose to believe in Christ, asked forgiveness for my sins and accepted that He died for me. But it took years for me to learn how to trust Him."

"What about all that stuff you're not supposed to do?"

He looked into her eager eyes. "It's not about a list of rules, Laura. God loves you for who you are, right now. Life isn't perfect. It'll never be perfect, but there's peace when you rest in the knowledge that God loved you enough to give up his Son so you can experience *real* life by trusting Him—forever."

She looked skeptical. "You don't blame God for taking away your wife?"

He sighed. "I don't know why God allowed that to happen, but He did. And there's been some good that's come out of it."

"Like what?"

"I'm building a relationship with my kids that's stronger than it's ever been. Since Joanne died, I realized what's important in this life. Family matters."

He watched her digest what he'd said, and then he went out on a limb. More than ever he wanted her to experience God. To find that peace. "We can pray right now if you're ready to make room for God in your life and in your heart."

Again she chewed her bottom lip, considering. And then she looked away. "I can't."

He lifted her chin, so she'd look at him. "It's something you need to do, Laura."

Tears filled her eyes. "It's hard to let go."

"I know, but it's the best decision you'll ever make." He wrestled with wanting to take her into his arms, but knew God was wooing her. He didn't want to get in the way.

"It's late." He lifted Harry out of her arms.

Laura sniffed, and then whispered, "Thanks, Jack, for caring enough to give me this chance."

His heart ricocheted inside his rib cage. "I care about you too much not to."

"Maybe another time." She smiled.

"Don't wait too long, Laura. Time's not always on our side."

Chapter Twelve

❧

"I just don't like any of them." Her mother sat on the living room floor with a pout forming on her lips.

Laura bit back a growl. They'd met with half a dozen home health aides and her mother had rejected every single one. It had been eight days since her mother had come home from the hospital, and Laura was more than ready to hightail it back to Wisconsin. "You're going to have to pick one of them, and soon."

"Why do I need one? I'm getting stronger. You said so yourself."

"Because I have to go back to work, and you need to continue with the therapy exercises. The doctor said so. I'll come home on the weekends as much as I can."

"That job holds you hostage. You won't come home."

"Mom, please." Her mother didn't understand the sense of accomplishment she derived from sealing a solid deal. Her job made her feel alive, worth something. Laura mattered at work.

"I'm sure you could sell computers in Houghton. With all those students at the colleges—"

"Mom, I *don't* sell computers," Laura said.

Her mother looked puzzled. "Then what do you sell?"

"Business solutions. We help businesses run better." Laura

gathered up the therapeutic exercise bands from the floor. There was no use finishing at this point. Besides, they needed to make food for their Labor Day family picnic. Peeling potatoes would be good therapy.

She'd been helping her mother with the exercises her physical therapist had shown her to improve her mother's left side. Hiring a P.T. trained home health aide was expensive, but it would alleviate trips to the Health Center three days a week.

"Sounds like a lot of smoke and mirrors if you ask me." Her mother followed her into the kitchen.

Laura bit her tongue. They'd had this conversation countless times. No matter how well Laura explained what she did, her mother liked to reduce it to selling computers.

"When do Jack and Angie get home?" Her mom put the teakettle on to boil.

Laura fumbled with the coffee can. Just hearing his name made her insides go soft. "I'm not sure."

They'd been gone four days, but Laura missed them. Bad.

"I hope they make it in time for the picnic." Her mom's voice sounded wistful.

Laura hoped they didn't. She didn't trust her feelings for Jack. She didn't want their reunion on display for the whole family. What if she did something stupid like show Jack how much she'd missed him?

"You're awfully quiet this morning." Her mom looked concerned.

Laura shrugged. "I've got a lot on my mind."

"Like what?"

Laura's hackles went up. "The home health aide working out, going back to work, just for starters."

Her mom's face fell. "If you're so anxious to leave, I'm not going to stop you."

"Mom, it's just that I want my life back." Her safety net. It wasn't her mom's fault that Laura didn't like pining after Jack.

Her mom looked hurt. "Don't you worry about me. I'll be fine."

"I know you will. Once we pick a home health aide, you'll be all set." She tried to sound positive.

"And you'll end up all alone if you don't watch out. You think Jack will wait around while you sell computers across the Midwest? You'll lose him just like you lost Anthony. No job's worth that, Laura." Her mother hobbled out the kitchen door onto the porch, taking her cup of tea with her.

Laura felt as if she'd been slapped. She'd been doing the best she could, trying to be careful for everyone's sake. No matter what she did, she couldn't seem to get it right.

Jack pulled into the driveway. Two other cars were parked near the house and three kids ran around screaming.

"Who's here?" Angie said.

"I guess we'll find out." He opened his door and Harry scooted out before he could catch him. The dog ran toward the porch, straight for Laura.

After spending four days away from her, he stared as if seeing her for the first time. Even in a baggy sweatshirt she looked classy, refined. Sweet. Her smile widened when she spotted him. Her hair blew across her face and she tucked it behind her ear as her gaze drilled into his.

Family disappeared, the noise of the kids and his packed truck faded to nothing. He saw only Laura.

She walked toward him with Harry in her arms. "Hi."

He wanted to take her in his arms, but this wasn't the time or the place. Not in front of everyone. Not when he didn't have a handle on the feelings running through him.

"You must be the doctor." A tall woman with bleached-blond hair and intent dark brown eyes stepped between them and held out her hand. "My mom, Nelda, told me about you. I'm Laura's cousin, Nancy."

The ladies had gathered around—Nelda, Mrs. Toivo and

cousin Nancy. They looked him over like a turkey under consideration for a Thanksgiving feast.

"Uh, I'm just a vet. My name's Jack and that's my daughter Angie." He caught the humor in Laura's eyes but also something close to jealousy shimmered when her cousin looked him over. Jack's heart pumped a little faster.

"That's still a lot of responsibility," Anna Toivo added.

Laura came to his rescue. "Okay, ladies, let Jack get settled in before you interrogate the poor guy."

He watched Anna, Nelda and Nancy head for the picnic table where they descended upon Angie. Angie didn't seem to mind, so he let her be. But Cousin Nancy kept glancing at him, along with a man who had to be Nelda's husband, Ed. He followed Laura to the back of his SUV and popped the hatch. "Thanks."

"I'll help you unload." She hoisted a sleeping bag over her shoulder and grabbed a duffel bag. "There's plenty of food if you and Angie want to join us, but don't feel like you have to if you're tired."

Jack smiled. Laura was the one who looked spent. "We'll hang out. Besides, I'm always hungry."

Her cheeks flushed, and she looked away. "How was Lansing?"

"Good. Ben and Angie caught up with their friends." He entered through the barn and unlocked the door to his apartment. "How was your weekend?"

"It was okay."

He dropped his suitcase on the floor then took the sleeping bag and duffel from Laura's hands and tossed them aside. He heard her gasp. "What is it?"

She held her finger. "It's just a scratch from the zipper of that duffel."

"Let me see." Jack reached for her.

"It's nothing." She dropped her hand at her side.

"Come on. I have bandages in the bathroom." Jack opened the medicine cabinet and rummaged for peroxide and a cotton ball. He expected Laura to follow him, but she remained still, standing in the middle of the floor. He gathered up the stuff and headed for the kitchen table.

"Have a seat, and I'll fix that cut."

She slipped into a chair with a sigh. "It's not a big deal."

He gave her an amused look of warning. "That's what they all say before infection sets in."

She smiled, but her eyes looked—scared.

He cupped her chin. "I'm teasing."

"I know."

He searched her troubled face. "What are you afraid of?"

Her eyes widened. "A lot of things, Jack."

Her skin was soft, silky. He knew better than to forge ahead, but that didn't mean he didn't want to. Especially after being away from her and realizing how much he cared.

He pulled his hand away and fumbled with the box of bandages while Laura proceeded to douse the cotton ball with peroxide. "I know."

"Ouch." She blew on her finger.

"Pretty nasty for a scratch." Jack used a napkin to pat dry the edge of her pinky finger. Then he gently applied the bandage.

"Jack—" Laura tried to pull her hand away.

Jack held on. "I missed you."

She didn't look away. She didn't speak, either, but her silence rang louder than words. Laura had missed him, too.

"It won't work. You and me. It won't."

His fingers twined through hers. "How do you know?"

She pulled away and stood. "Let's leave this alone. It's better for everyone if we stay friends. Nothing more."

Jack knew she was right. His brain wrapped around her current priorities, and her precarious journey toward faith. Those two things alone demanded that he back off. But the rest of him wanted to show her what lurked in his heart. He couldn't. He wouldn't.

Not yet.

Laura was the last to dig into the food. She plopped a spoonful of her mother's potato salad onto a paper plate.

"Are you going to tell me about Doctor Gorgeous?" Nancy ladled pickles onto her hamburger.

"There's nothing to tell."

"Spare me," Nancy groaned. "You two took your time unloading that SUV. He's aware of your every move and you look flustered. What gives?"

Laura squeezed the ketchup bottle too hard, sending a blob across her hot dog. "I told you. It's nothing."

Nancy shook her head. "You're going to leave that big hunk of man and go back to Wisconsin?"

Laura looked at her cousin. "I have a job, Nancy. A life. Besides, it's complicated."

"With you, it's always complicated. You're not getting any younger, you know, Laura."

"Since when is thirty-one ancient?" Laura skewered her cousin with a glare. She felt like someone had scrubbed her down with sandpaper—all raw and prickly.

"Whatever happened to getting married right after college, having kids and living in a big farmhouse? Isn't that what you used to want?"

Laura shrugged. As teenagers, she'd told Nancy that she wanted tons of kids, so no child of hers would grow up alone. Her children could make cookies, have friends over and she wouldn't worry about the mess. She'd never be like her mother. But Laura was every bit as alone as her mother, maybe more so. "I grew up."

"You ran away." Nancy grabbed a handful of chips.

No matter what Laura thought of her cousin's life when it came to staying in the area and selecting a spouse, Nancy *was* a good mother. Her kids were rambunctious but sweet. "I changed my mind about what I wanted out of life. What's so terrible about that?"

"Not a thing." Nancy didn't look convinced.

Laura wasn't, either. When it came to relationships, Laura hadn't found success. Maybe she never would.

"He's a looker," Nancy said as she eyed Jack.

"Yeah."

"Then go for it, Laura. He seems like a nice guy."

"He is." She considered the gentle care Jack gave her puny cut, the feel of his hand holding hers. *Nice* didn't quite do the man justice.

"Grab the happiness while you can." Nancy's tone sounded wistful, as if happiness was too fleeting to last.

"Thanks, Nancy. It's something to think about."

"Don't think too long." Nancy winked at her and then joined the others.

Laura squelched the urge to make a face. Instead, she watched her cousin fuss over her kids, cutting a hot dog into little pieces, blowing on a hot ear of corn, and generally taking care of them.

Laura wasn't used to caring for others. She couldn't claim patience in waiting out her mother's recovery. She wanted her old life back. Her independence.

And yet Jack had been thrust into the sole caregiver role when his wife died. He hadn't much of a choice, but he'd met the challenge with selflessness. He put his kids first, she could tell. There was a steady security about him. Stability.

It suddenly dawned on Laura that Anthony had been looking for someone to take over his responsibility with Brooke rather than share it. Someone to keep his daughter busy when it was his turn with shared custody. Jack would never expect that. Moving here was about meeting the needs of his daughter and being near his son. His decision. His loving burden. One he'd never shirk.

She stared at the jar of pickle relish far too long. Balancing her plate, she grabbed a lawn chair and pulled it next to her aunt.

Aunt Nelda leaned toward her. "Ed and I were just telling Jack about you and Nancy as kids. You two tried to outdo the other, which usually got you both into trouble."

Laura laughed. "Oh no."

Her mother clicked her tongue. "All Laura ever said was that Nancy had this and Nancy had that. I wasn't made of money. We were on a fixed income."

Laura's smile slipped. She'd always wondered why her mother didn't get a job to fill her time once Laura was in high school. She'd even tried to encourage her mother by leaving the classifieds on the table with fun-sounding jobs circled in red. But her mother never went to a single interview. Her mother said that she didn't want Laura getting off the bus to an empty house.

"Oh, Anna, little girls are meant to be spoiled," Aunt Nelda said.

"One time…" Her aunt then launched into a tale about rescuing Laura and Nancy after they'd been caught sneaking into the movie theater without paying.

And so it began. The pain of childhood memories retold for Jack. Each story was punctuated by her mother's complaints.

Laura grabbed the empty iced tea pitcher. "I'll be back."

Jack watched her go. Something was wrong. He listened with half an ear to Aunt Nelda's rambling story. Angie soaked in every detail with bright eyes and he hoped she didn't get any ideas. Nancy's kids played with their food. No one would miss him. He didn't care if they did.

"I'll get more ice." Jack was on his feet. He caught Nancy's knowing look when he grabbed the ice bucket and gave her a nod.

When he stepped through the kitchen, the ticking of the clock on the wall was all he heard above the laughter from the picnic drifting through the opened windows. "Laura?"

He heard movement upstairs. He set the bucket on the counter. "Laura, are you up here?"

When she opened the door to the bathroom, he felt like an idiot, until he saw her puffy eyes.

"What is it?"

"Nothing." She waved her hand.

He opened his arms, and after a moment's hesitation, she stepped into them. "Tell me."

"It'll take too long," she said into his chest.

He kissed her hair. "Is it your mom?"

Laura broke apart from him. "When I'm gone, I figure it's never as bad as I make it out to be, and then after I'm here awhile, I know why I hate coming home."

Jack had felt helpless when Joanne cried, but watching Laura fight down her tears was worse. Laura didn't battle crying, she looked like she fought her feelings. "Maybe you need to talk about it."

She leaned against the doorjamb. "Like I said before, I don't think my mother wanted kids, but I came along when she was forty-three. I was my dad's little princess. He used to call me that even though my mother didn't like it. I think she was jealous of me. There wasn't anything weird between my dad and me, it was just that Mom wanted Dad all to herself."

He folded his arms and just listened.

"My dad died when I was twelve." Her voice lowered.

"He was my partner in crime—that's what he used to say when we'd sneak my mom's cookie dough. I thought maybe Mom and I would get closer, in our grief at least. But she shut me out. She was so lost herself she didn't bother to help me. I tried to make her happy, anything to…" Her voice caught and broke.

"You were just a kid."

She looked at him, her eyes wide and full of hurt. "Nothing I ever did made a difference and that hasn't changed. I can't do anything to please her. It took all week to find a health aide she'd accept. I took her to her appointments and never once did she thank me for helping out. Maybe I'm being a baby, but is it so hard to say thank you?"

"It shouldn't be."

Laura sniffed. "Why does she needle me every time I'm home?"

Jack cocked his head. "Maybe she doesn't know how to handle missing you."

"Maybe."

Jack didn't know what else to say. "Have you talked to her?"

Laura stuck both her hands through her hair as if she wanted to pull it out. "I've tried, but it doesn't do any good. Do you see why I can't stay here? If I stay too long, I'd turn into that kid who tries too hard. I tried all week and I'm done. I just can't do it anymore."

Jack felt his gut tighten. He couldn't fix this. Only God could. If Laura would let Him.

"I'm sorry to unload on you like this." Her short bark of laughter was laced with bitterness.

"I'm glad you told me. Anything I can do?"

"No. But thanks for listening."

He was helpless. After all she'd done for Angie, he couldn't offer a single solution. At least not one she looked willing to accept. "Anytime."

"I've got iced tea to make." She blew past him and charged down the stairs.

Silently, Jack cracked ice while Laura made another pitcher of tea. As she stirred the powder into the water, he could tell she was stuffing her hurt back inside as if preparing to take on the second half of a losing game. She even laughed when he sent ice cubes flying all over the counter.

Being away from her for four days, Jack felt like part of him was missing. Left behind. He'd thought about her nonstop. He'd prayed for her. Even his sister had asked why he'd been preoccupied.

He'd given a lame excuse about getting the vet practice books in order and on the computer. He wasn't about to admit that he was falling for a woman who wasn't a believer and valued work before family. Laura lacked the two most important qualities he looked for in a woman.

Before he'd even broached the subject of her staying, she admitted she couldn't wait to leave. And it sounded too much like she didn't want to come back. At what point could he pursue a relationship with Laura? Now wasn't the time. It might never be the right time. He had to accept that and let it go. He had to let her go.

Chapter Thirteen

"Come on, Ange. The bus will be here any minute." Jack rinsed the last of the breakfast dishes while Angie finished getting ready.

The frustrated sound he heard confirmed she was nervous. The first day at a new school. The worst. He'd offered to drive her, but she refused, saying she might as well get used to riding the bus. Her face-it-head-on attitude filled him with pride. She wasn't the same despairing little girl he'd brought from Lansing. And Laura had played a big role in that change.

Laura.

She was back to her usual smiling self even as she took her mom into Hancock yesterday. She'd been close to his thoughts and the subject of his prayers. She had a world of hurt balled up inside of her. No wonder she understood Angie.

The bathroom door opened and Angie wore the new outfit she picked out with Laura. There was no trace of the tomboy today. Boys were bound to notice. He folded his arms.

"What?" Angie cocked her head to the side.

Jack grinned. "You look very pretty."

She rolled her eyes and headed for the door. Harry followed, sniffing the cuff of her jeans.

"See, Harry thinks so, too." Jack followed her out.

They stood by the side of the road. Chicory dotted the grassy ditch and the cornflower-blue petals flickered in the breeze. He glanced at Angie who fiddled with her backpack. "Got everything, your cell phone?"

"Yep," she said quickly.

"Lunch money?"

"Yes." She sounded irritated.

"Call me if you need anything. The school office has my cell, and the vet office number, too."

Angie dropped her head back. "I know, Dad."

Jack held up his hands. "Okay, okay."

Angie stared down the road, twisting the strap of her backpack.

"Want to pray real quick?" He thought for sure she'd refuse, but instead she nodded. Jack kept his expression serious even though he felt like jumping for joy.

They both bowed their heads. "Dear Lord, please protect Angie today, and let her meet some good friends. Amen."

"Amen," she whispered.

Jack heard the sound of a bus chugging down the road before he saw the blinking red lights. He looked back at Angie. She looked scared. The dog sat calmly at her feet, as if sensing that now was not a time to play.

As the bus drew closer, Jack squeezed Angie's shoulder. "I love you, sweetheart."

"Thanks, Dad. You, too."

The bus stopped and his little girl got on. Only she wasn't so little anymore. Harry sat at Jack's feet as he waved. Angie waved back then clamored into a seat beside an animated blond girl. She'd do just fine.

Laura dropped the lace curtains into place. Her heart nearly burst as she watched Jack and Angie waiting for the bus. Seeing them pray together warmed her soul. They'd come so far in such a short time. They didn't need her anymore, which was just as well. Jack and Angie would be just fine after she left.

Imagining Jack's simple prayer, she remembered how her dad used to wait with her to catch the bus before he headed to work at the mill. Her cell rang, shattering the memory. "Hello?"

"Hey, Laura, it's Cindy. I hate to bug you, but I need your help."

Laura's heart sank at her assistant's worried tone. Two major contracts were renewing and her manager wouldn't approve the concessions Laura had made. The clients were planning to walk.

Laura gritted her teeth. "You told Jeff we'd lose the account?"

"He's at corporate the rest of this week. Susan said if she approves it, she's taking the account."

The office floundered into cutthroat territory without their sales manager, but Laura wasn't about to give up two clients. "I'll call them and stall until I can meet with them personally. I need to meet with Mr. Albertson about his management retreat. Can you set that up? And Cindy, would you like to attend this retreat with me next weekend?"

"Absolutely, Laura. Thanks, I knew you'd come through."

Laura felt the familiar glow of being needed, of success in finding a solution to the problem. She couldn't wait to get back to work.

After she hung up with Cindy, Laura found her mom in the kitchen wearing an apron and rolling little balls of dough through cinnamon sugar. "What are you doing?"

"Angie's going to need cookies when she gets home after her first day in a new school." Her mom's head was down, engrossed in flattening the dough balls on the cookie sheet.

"That's nice of you."

Her mom shrugged her shoulders. "The therapist said I needed to work my left hand."

"Do you want help?" She was proud of her mother for not

giving in to the stroke. It meant she'd move on, which meant Laura could, too.

Her mom swatted her with a towel. "Wash your hands."

Some things never changed. "Jack loves homemade cookies, but chocolate chip are his favorite."

"He'll have to make do with snicker doodles." Her mom rolled another ball. "These were your father's favorites."

"I didn't know that."

"Cookies and a cup of coffee, that's all he ever wanted no matter how many cakes or pies I made."

She glanced at her mom. "Do you still miss him?"

Her mom's brow furrowed and her eyes looked mistier than they did a moment ago. "I miss him more now than the year he died."

Laura swallowed hard. She didn't trust herself to talk. Her mother was alone and had been for years. It was supposed to get easier as time passed, not harder.

"What about you?" Her mom flattened more coated balls of dough into thick circles on another cookie sheet.

"More so when I'm here." She looked at her mom, feeling closer to her than she had in a long time. "It never goes away, does it?"

"Unless you fill it with something else, it only gets worse." She patted Laura's hand then took the cookie sheets and placed them in the hot oven and set the timer.

"Don't let them burn." Her mother waddled into the downstairs bathroom and shut the door.

Laura stared after her. Jack got through his wife's death by filling it with his faith. Laura had run to a life and career away from home. But what had her mother done? She had nothing to fill the void her father's death had left in their lives.

She could have filled it with me.

Tears stung the corners of her eyes at the unbidden thought. Why didn't her mother take an active interest in her own daughter's life? She'd always treated Laura as if she'd been a burden. An ungrateful, noisy, messy teenager.

Her mom baked cookies for Angie just like she'd done for Laura all those years ago. A pang of regret laced through her. She'd never appreciated those cookies, or considered what they might have meant.

Her mother wasn't demonstrative in her affection like her dad had been. She just wasn't a warm, fuzzy kind of person, but she'd always baked for her. How often had Laura misread her mother's actions? All these years, she'd wanted her to behave like her father. Cuddle her, read to her, love her. But her mother wasn't wired that way.

Jack's comment about her mother's way of showing that she missed Laura resonated. Was her mom's nagging a misguided sign of affection?

Laura came back to life with a start when the timer went off. Slipping on an oven mitt, she pulled the cookie sheets out and set them on the stovetop. They were perfect. Too bad life wasn't that easy.

Jack cut out of work early in order to meet Angie when she got off the bus. Followed by a shorter girl about Angie's age, Harry circled the girls, barking and wagging his tail.

After petting Harry, Angie introduced her friend. "Dad, this is Melissa. Can she stay for a while?"

Jack eyed the blonde-haired girl. She looked like a good kid. "Hi, Melissa. Have you checked with your mom?"

"We just moved in down the road." Melissa flipped open a tiny cell phone. "But she's probably at church."

He liked the sound of that. He watched Melissa dial and her movements reminded him of Laura when she called her office. It didn't matter where he was or what he did, thoughts of Laura hit him from everywhere.

"She wants to talk to you," Melissa said.

He took the impossibly tiny phone and introduced himself. After a short conversation, he found out that Melissa's family had bought Carl's place. Small world.

He handed back the phone. "She'll pick you up at five, right after her youth group meeting. So, ladies, how was the first day of school?"

Angie shrugged her shoulders.

Melissa wasn't so reticent. "It's so nice not going to a huge junior high school. I think I'm going to really like it here, with all the water and real snow. My brother likes to ski and so does my dad. Angie said you live in an apartment attached to a barn? That is so cool."

Jack grinned, but his daughter looked embarrassed. "Come on, it won't take long to show you around."

Before they could make it inside, Laura and her mom pulled into the drive. He waved.

Laura waved back and helped her mom out of the car.

Anna looked spry in powder-blue sweats and sneakers. She called out with a strong voice, "Come over for cookies with the girls."

"We'll be there after the grand tour," Jack said.

"She made cookies?" Angie asked. "Sweet."

Looking around their small apartment, Jack knew he needed to attend to building a house before renovations for a vet facility could start. Angie needed more space and where was he going to put Ben during breaks?

"Are you coming, Dad?" Angie asked at the door. Harry looked ready to follow them to Anna's.

"Harry, stay." Jack laughed when the dog went to his bed and lay down with a groan.

Melissa giggled. "Now that we live in the country, I hope we can get a dog. Maybe even a horse."

"My dad's going to get us some horses. I can't wait. We

already fixed the fence, so it's just a matter of finding a couple good ones for sale," Angie said.

Jack listened to the girls chatter as they walked across the yard. Perhaps Angie could get involved in 4-H. It'd be a good way to keep his daughter busy. He didn't want her languishing into boredom, which usually led to trouble with boys.

He didn't want to think about his daughter and boys, but knew he couldn't keep his head in the sand on that subject forever. One of these days, they'd have to have the *dating* talk. He shuddered at the thought, grateful there was plenty of time yet.

Jack knocked on the screen door.

"Come in," Laura called from inside.

Jack's heart did a little flip. He couldn't stop himself from reacting to her, wishing there was a way for them. "Laura, meet Angie's friend, Melissa. Her family moved here from Indianapolis."

"Hello, Melissa. Indy? This must be a big change for you."

Melissa flipped her hair. "Yeah, but Dad got a great job opportunity at the hospital."

Jack caught Laura's questioning glance and tried not to laugh. Precocious was too small a word when it came to Angie's friend.

"This is my mom, Mrs. Toivo. She made the cookies."

Anna smiled at the girls, patting an empty chair next to her. Angie took it, and Melissa sat across from Angie.

"Want some coffee?" Laura asked.

"If you're making it." He leaned against the kitchen sink and watched her move about the kitchen. When she filled the coffee pot with water, he leaned close and whispered, "How was your day?"

Her cheeks went pink and she bumped into him as she stepped back, sloshing water on the floor.

"Oh, Laura, be careful," said her mother.

"I got it, Mrs. T. I was in her way." Jack grabbed a handful of paper towels and mopped up the spill.

Laura kept busy.

He wanted to tell Laura about his day at the vet office and show her his progression in getting the books on the computer. He'd ordered a tablet PC in Houghton, but it hadn't come in yet. He wanted to pick her business-solutions brain, ask her how to keep track of inventories better, meds and supplies. He'd love to go over his ideas about relocating the practice, get her feedback. She'd have some pointers for him. Things to consider.

This wasn't an excuse to be near her. He needed her help.

Yeah, right.

Laura handed him the plate of cookies.

Jack took two. "You made these, Anna? They're delicious."

Anna's smile grew. "Thank you."

After a discussion about the girls' first day at school, coffee and a few more cookies, Jack rose to his feet. "Well girls, let's thank these ladies and be on our way."

"Thank you, Mrs. Toivo," Angie said.

"You're welcome, dear." Anna smiled.

"Yeah, and thanks, Mrs. Stahl," Melissa said.

Jack halted. His ears grew hot and his insides tingled as he glanced at a flustered Laura.

"Oh no, I'm not Mrs. Stahl," Laura stuttered.

Melissa looked confused.

Jack's tongue wouldn't work.

Angie saved the day. "My dad and Laura aren't married. We bought the barn from Laura's mom."

Melissa looked at Jack and shrugged. "Oh, sorry."

"No problem." But Jack's pulse raced.

The girls scrambled out the door.

"Why don't you come back and eat dinner with us," Laura's mom said before Jack could leave.

He needed to get his bearings. The idea of marrying Laura had knocked him senseless. "Thanks, Anna, but we're trying out a new church tonight at seven."

"We bought all this food in town. Besides, I have to work my left side and cooking will do that. Why don't you and Angie come back about five-thirty? That way, you can still make it to church on time."

He took a deep breath and glanced at Laura. "Is that okay with you?"

"Sure." Laura shrugged. She still looked stunned. Maybe, she was thinking the same things as he.

He'd love to know. Laura had paled white as a sheet when Melissa had called her Mrs. Stahl. An honest mistake, but one that clarified everything. The feelings Jack had tried to ignore bulldozed their way to the front of the line where denial wasn't an option. He had to admit the truth. To himself at least.

He loved Laura.

"Jack?" Laura asked.

"Yeah. Five-thirty." He looked at Anna who stared back with amusement shining from her eyes. Did it show? He let the screen door close with a snap.

God, what do I do now?

Chapter Fourteen

Laura was aware of Jack watching her as she cleared the dinner dishes. Heat flushed her cheeks when she bent near him to grab the bowl of potatoes. He'd been quiet during the meal, thoughtful. She'd caught him looking at her several times, as if considering something.

"Well, ladies, sorry to eat and run. We're checking out Melissa's Wednesday night church service. They have an active youth group." Jack pushed back his chair and stood. "I hate to leave you with this mess."

"It's no trouble. Go and have a good time." Laura's mom cradled a hot cup of tea, her usual end to a heavy meal.

"Would you two like to join us? We can help with the dishes afterward."

"No, thanks," Laura answered before her mother could. Church in the middle of the week? Ick. She grabbed the tub of margarine and headed for the fridge.

Jack touched her elbow, stopping her cold. "Come with me on Sunday then."

She looked into his pleading eyes and her resolve melted. What could it hurt? "Okay."

"Great." He let his hand glide across her forearm, leaving behind a trail of warmth. "You, too, Mrs. T."

Her mom nodded. "Sounds good to me."

"Thanks again for dinner," Jack said before slipping out the door.

Laura gathered up the rest of the dishes, while her mother waddled to the sink. "Don't worry, Mom. I can do these. Why don't you go in and watch TV."

"I can help." Her mother wasn't going to be put off. She slopped a soapy dishcloth against a plate. "Jack's sweet on you."

Laura laughed. "Why's that?"

"He asked you to church."

Laura smiled at her mother's attempt to tease. "He asked you, too."

As she dried a dish, Laura didn't know what to feel. All she knew was that being around Jack affected her deeply. Getting back to work next week would no doubt put things in perspective. If she stayed home much longer, she might lose her focus. That was something she couldn't afford to risk, not now.

Friday morning, Laura's cell phone woke her up. "Hello?"

"Laura, it's Cindy."

She sat up and checked the clock. Eight-thirty. She was turning into a late riser since coming home. "What's up?"

"Corporate called. They want to see you Monday for an interview."

Laura ran a shaking hand through her hair. "What?"

"You're in contention for one of the senior sales exec positions. Congratulations."

Laura couldn't catch her breath. She jotted down the details. She'd catch a plane to St. Louis first thing Monday morning from Madison. Which meant she needed to leave this weekend. Not today, though. The home health aide was coming for the first time, and Laura promised her mother she'd be here.

She threw back her covers and jumped out of bed. Her heart raced. This is what she'd worked so hard for. The culmination of years spent proving herself worthy of the opportunity. She had to prepare.

"Laura?" Her mom's voice carried up the stairs into her room.

"What is it?" She called out of her opened door.

"Aren't we going to do my exercises?"

Laura took a deep breath before answering. They'd gone over this last night at dinner. Jack and Angie had made other plans, but their absence made the table feel vacant somehow.

"Laura?"

"Mom, we're going to do your exercises with the aide. I'll be down in a minute, okay?"

Laura quickly showered and dressed. She made it downstairs in time to help her mother make oatmeal and sliced fruit for breakfast. She'd made some headway in getting her mother to eat a little healthier.

Once they were seated, Laura broached the subject of leaving a couple days earlier than expected. "Mom, I got a call this morning from work."

Her mother held her spoon in midair before settling it back into her bowl. Her expression hardened. "They need you back."

"I've got an interview Monday at corporate for a promotion. Isn't that great?" Laura grinned.

Her mother's eyes narrowed. "When will you leave?"

Laura sprinkled more sugar on her oatmeal. "Tomorrow, I guess."

"But you promised Jack you'd go to church with him on Sunday."

"I'll go another time."

"Oh, Laura, don't start doing that to him."

She cocked her head. "Doing what?"

"Breaking promises."

"Mom, this is important." Why couldn't she be happy for her?

"For Jack, attending his church service with him is important. I can tell."

Laura knew her mother was right. The look in Jack's eyes when he'd asked her confirmed it. "There'll be other services."

Her mother shook her head. "What if there's not?"

"Come on, Mom. I'll be gone a week. I can go next Sunday."

"I know you're an adult, but I'm still your mother. You need to go to service *this* Sunday. You can leave afterward and still get to your condo at a decent hour."

Laura's jaw dropped. "But I have to prepare for this interview."

Her mother sighed. "Why can't you do that here?"

"When?" Laura couldn't keep the surliness from her voice. They had a full day planned, including a trip to the hairdresser so her mother could get her hair cut.

"Tomorrow. Take the whole day, I don't care, but make time to go to church with Jack."

"I want this job, Mom. Why are you giving me a hard time?"

Her mother's gaze bore into hers. "Are you sure this is what you really want?"

Since when did her mother know anything about her wishes? Laura got up from the table and put her bowl in the sink. "Of course it's what I want. I've wanted it forever."

Grabbing her tennis shoes, she headed for the door. "I'm going for a walk. I need some fresh air."

Laura slipped onto the porch and into her shoes. The breeze felt cool and the sky blazed without a single cloud. She stepped into the grass and Harry appeared before her and dropped a ball at her feet.

"What do you want?" The dog demanded yet another thing Laura felt ill equipped to give. She couldn't throw far.

Harry wagged his tail and barked.

With a groan, she picked up the ball. And then she spotted Jack walking toward her. Her heart did its usual flutter.

"I'm taking the dog for a walk before work, want to come with us?"

"That's where I was going."

Harry barked again, reminding her what he wanted.

She threw the ball a pitiful distance, and then fell into step with Jack. "How was dinner at Melissa's last night?"

"They're nice people. Angie liked the youth service. They have a group outing Saturday night and she's excited about going."

"That's great."

"I think we've found what we're looking for in a church. I think you'll like it, too." Jack squinted against the sun. She loved the way his eyes crinkled at the corners. He threw the ball for Harry this time, and the dog jumped like a spring toy through the tall grass.

Laura couldn't bring herself to tell him she wasn't going.

They walked in silence until they came to the pasture and ducked under the barbed wire. Laura slipped her hand into Jack's as he helped her up. "You did a nice job of fixing the fence."

"I'd like to replace it with white split rail eventually. Until then, I'll keep mending fences."

Laura smiled. He was good at that. Mending his relationship with Angie, even mending Laura's relationship with her mom. It was easier when Jack and Angie were around. More fun, too.

Jack tucked a fine strand of Laura's blond hair behind her ear. "What's going on?"

Laura looked into his kind blue eyes. "What do you mean?"

"You look troubled."

She took a deep breath. "I have an interview for a promotion on Monday."

He gave her a quick bear hug, then stepped back. "Congratulations, that's great."

"Thanks." Laura looked at the grass.

He lifted her chin. "So, what's wrong?"

She shrugged. "I need to prepare. It's in St. Louis at our corporate headquarters."

He whistled. "Nervous?"

She didn't know what she felt. Her mother's reaction had put a damper on the excitement level. And the thought of letting Jack down if she didn't go with him to church wasn't helping, either. Maybe it was just nerves making her grumpy. "Yeah."

Jack grinned. "Can I help? We can role play."

She laughed. She couldn't imagine Jack asking her about sales plans and cold calling. But he was sweet for offering. "Thanks, but I think I can handle it with some alone time."

Harry dropped the ball at Jack's feet and barked.

Jack threw it even farther. He moved with smooth, athletic grace.

Laura grinned at far that ball went. "Nice throw."

"I should have been a quarterback instead of a tight end in high school. But I was afraid of hurting my arm. I played baseball in the spring."

"A big tough guy like you afraid of getting hurt?" She flashed him a cocky grin.

"You know what they say, the bigger they are, the harder they fall."

"Who's the pansy now, Dr. Stahl?"

"I'll show you who's the pansy." Jack darted for her.

Laura wasn't about to stick around to find out what Jack might do. She took off running.

Jack chased after her, but Harry joined in the fun. Barking, the little dog tangled around Jack's legs, causing him to stumble.

She heard Jack scold the dog just before he fell, taking her down as if he'd tackled her. They landed in a heap.

At first, she couldn't catch her breath.

"Laura?"

But then an idea spread through her with ornery pleasure.

Jack wasn't the only one who could tease. She lay perfectly still and kept her eyes closed.

He gently shook her shoulder. "Laura?"

She tried not to laugh when she felt Jack's fingers brush her forehead.

"Come on, baby doll, wake up."

She heard the panic in his voice, but her lips twitched. She couldn't torture the poor guy any longer. "What kind of a lame nickname is that?"

He dropped his forehead against hers. "Cute, real cute."

"No, really, I want to know." She laughed when Harry dropped the ball next to her ear.

Jack propped himself on his elbow and threw the ball for the dog. "It just came out. I've never called anyone that before, but it suits you."

"Why?"

He looked like he might explain, but then he shook his head. "Forget it."

"Nice tackle by the way," she whispered.

His eyes took on an intensity she hadn't seen before. "You owe me."

"I do not."

"You scared me half to death. I say you do."

"What do you want?" Her voice came out raspy. A relationship with Jack would be yet another demand on her time, and her heart. But she couldn't ignore her feelings for him any longer. Deep down, she didn't want to.

The closer he leaned toward her, the more her heart raced. Laura felt the erratic beats deep inside her chest. It didn't help that his hand rubbed from her elbow to her shoulder and back.

They stared at each other a moment longer. Maybe two.

Jack needed to regain his balance and quick. His breathing wasn't steady, either. Now was his chance to do something. If he let Laura return to Wisconsin without any attempt to let her know about his interest, he'd regret it.

He took a deep breath. "How about a date tomorrow night. Maybe the movies?"

Her eyes clouded over and, for a minute, Jack thought she'd refuse. But then she smiled, her blue eyes shining. "That'd be nice."

He'd asked her out. And she'd accepted. Now they were getting somewhere.

Saturday evening arrived and Laura was running late. After spending the majority of the day at the college in Houghton preparing for her interview, Laura knew a movie was just the thing to take her mind off the doubts chewing up her confidence.

Settling for jeans and a button-down shirt, Laura checked her makeup in the mirror. She charged down the stairs and found her mom in the living room watching the news. "I should be back by ten or eleven at the latest. You've got my cell number and Jack's if you need anything."

"I'll be fine. Have a good time." Her mom sat in her easy chair with her tea and a magazine. She never looked happier to see Laura heading out the door. Of course, going out with Jack had everything to do with that.

Laura had actually listened to her mom. And maybe, she'd been right. Laura was ready for Monday. Going out with Jack, and even attending church tomorrow would keep her occupied. By the time she got home to her condo, she'd pack her bags and get a good night's sleep. No time for pacing the floor.

"Thanks, Mom." Laura took a calming breath and left with a snap of the screen door as it closed.

Jack met her in the middle of the driveway. He gave her a slow smile of appreciation and Laura's insides flipped. "Your car or mine?"

They were taking the next step. A real date. It was just the movies. They'd have fun and keep it simple.

"Let's take mine. We can put the top down."

The twenty-mile distance to the Houghton movie theater passed in a blur of talking about everything and nothing. When they arrived, they wound their way through the crowd, bought tickets and popcorn, and found seats in the middle of the row.

Settling into the seats, Laura placed her drink in the cup holder.

Jack pushed back the divider turning their chairs into something like a love seat. Without any pretense, he draped his arm around her shoulders. "Much better."

"You think?" She squeaked while reaching into his bucket of popcorn.

"Don't you?"

"I can't breathe." She made light of it, even though sitting close to him made it true. Going on a date with Jack was fun, exhilarating, and complicated everything.

He leaned close. "Don't worry, I'm trained in CPR."

A delicious shiver surged up her spine. The lights were still on and people poured in around them. They were safe. "Maybe later."

He laughed, a deep rumbling she felt through her arm plastered against his side. "Definitely, later."

Laura took a sip of her diet pop to quell the sensation of her bones turning to jelly, when she heard kids from behind them.

"Angie, isn't that your dad?" Melissa's familiar voice asked.

Laura turned and looked. Two rows back, Laura caught the expression on Angie's face. She looked horrified, embarrassed and angry didn't quite do her justice.

Laura cringed. She wished she could materialize into a different movie theater—in fact anywhere else would do. She offered up an apologetic smile but it didn't help. The kid looked straight through her.

"It's the youth group outing," Jack said with a soft groan. He stood and addressed Angie and Melissa then joked with a couple of the boys. He also shook hands with the youth minister.

Laura watched, but remained seated. She hoped Jack didn't introduce her. Her cheeks flushed as she waved at Melissa, who wore an I-knew-it smile. Their first date was on display for Angie's entire youth group.

Jack settled back down next to her.

"Don't you dare put your arm around me," she whispered.

"Why?"

"Your daughter is not happy to see us."

She felt Jack shrug. "Of course not, who wants your dad showing up at the same place where you're with friends."

"It's more than that, Jack."

"Don't worry about it." He clasped her hand with his.

Laura clenched her teeth. Worry? She knew that look. She'd seen it hundreds of times from Anthony's daughter, Brooke. Hadn't she learned her lesson? Never come between a man and his daughter.

After the movie, Laura watched as the theater emptied. She dreaded facing Angie, but didn't have a choice when Jack caught up with the kids. "I'll see you at home, Ange. Have fun."

Angie nodded and ran ahead.

"Would you like some ice cream?" Jack asked.

"I ate too much popcorn."

He smiled. "There's always room for ice cream."

Within ten minutes they were sitting at a café table outside a small ice cream shop. Laura had succumbed to a scoop of cherry royale. "Maybe this isn't a good idea."

"I can finish yours." Jack licked his waffle cone.

"I don't mean the ice cream, I mean us, dating."

He jerked his head to look at her. "Why?"

"Look at Angie's reaction."

"You're making too much of it. I'll talk to her."

"What will you do if she's not okay with this, with us seeing each other?"

Jack expression was serious, even though he took his daughter's glares this evening lightly. "We'll figure it out."

Laura needed to make Jack understand. "Remember when I told you I'd been engaged?"

"Yeah."

"Anthony called it quits because his daughter wouldn't accept me no matter how hard I tried. I can't deal with that heartache again, Jack. I won't."

He covered Laura's hand with his own. "I'm not Anthony."

But what if Angie reacted like Brooke?

The door slammed shut as Jack's daughter stormed into the apartment and stomped up the stairs to her room.

Jack looked up from his paperwork. He'd been home for only half an hour. "I know you're mad, Angie, so you can kill the drama."

"Why'd you have to go to the movies?" she yelled down.

"Why not the movies?"

Angie made an exasperated growling sound. "Didn't you hear me say that *we* were going to the movies tonight?"

Jack wasn't sure what made her so angry. She hadn't said a thing about him being there with Laura. "I'm not going to shout. If you want to talk about this, you'll have to come downstairs."

After a few minutes, she came down the twisting iron staircase and sat on the bottom step. "I told you the youth group was going to the movies in Houghton."

"I didn't hear you."

"That's because you weren't listening." Angie cocked her head and she looked just like her mother. She sounded like Joanne, too.

Jack wasn't about to be scolded by his thirteen-year-old. "You want to tell me what's really bothering you? What's the big deal with me showing up at the same movie?"

Angie threw her head back and stared at the ceiling as if he was beyond understanding. "Because it wasn't just you."

"Do you have a problem with me spending time with Laura?"

She shot him an annoyed look. "When were you going to tell me that you asked her out? Shouldn't I know that?"

Jack swallowed hard. He should have told her. Instead, he'd taken the coward's route. He'd left Angie a note, in case she got home first, making it appear like it was a spur-of-the-moment thing, not the planned date it truly was. And God wasn't letting him get away with that deception.

"You're right, I should have told you. Are you upset that I asked Laura out?"

Angie looked at her bare feet planted firmly on the plank floor. "Dad, everyone kept asking me who was she? Was she my mom? Was she your girlfriend or what? The guys kept teasing—saying she was gorgeous. I didn't need that."

Jack sighed. Finally understanding how awkward it must have been for her. He'd put her in the situation unprepared. "I'm sorry, sweetheart."

She looked up, her stare hard and seeking. "So what's the deal?"

He took a deep breath. How much should he tell her? What was the protocol? He'd never, ever been in this spot before. He decided on brevity. "Tonight was our first date."

Not exactly the best of dates.

Angie looked like she was trying to read between the lines of the obvious. Her eyebrows lifted. "And?"

He wasn't getting off that easy. "I'd like to ask her out again, and I need to know how you feel about it."

Angie rested her chin in the palm of her hand, considering. "Ben says you like her a lot."

Since when did Ben know anything about it? "Look, Ange, you and Ben come first with me, always. But I want Laura to be my girlfriend."

He cringed. Girlfriend? It sounded completely juvenile. But he'd put his goal out there and let Angie know his intent was serious.

"What about Mom?"

Jack hesitated. He wanted to move on, but maybe Angie wasn't ready. What if she wouldn't accept someone else taking Joanne's place in his life. "Ange, no matter what I feel for Laura, that won't ever change my love for your mom."

Angie eyes filled with tears.

His throat felt tight, too. He cleared it. "I miss your mom, Angie. but I don't want to spend the rest of my life alone. Laura's worried that you don't want us going out again. If that's true, we're going to have to figure out a way to deal with it. Is that fair?"

Angie nodded. She looked so forlorn, as if realizing for the first time that he wasn't just her dad. He was a flesh-and-blood person with feelings like anyone else.

"Just think about it, okay? No pressure to tell me right now."

"Okay."

"Am I forgiven for being a dumb dad?"

A wispy smile hovered at her lips. "Yeah."

"I love you, Angie. That won't ever change."

"I love you, too, Dad." But Angie didn't leave. She sat on the bottom step, tracing the outline of the wrought-iron handrail with her finger.

"What is it?"

"Did Laura think I was mad at her?"

Jack's heart swelled with pride. "I don't know, honey. Were you?"

Angie shrugged.

"Laura cares about you. It wouldn't hurt to let her know that you care for her back."

Angie nodded, looking miserable. "Good night, Dad."

"Good night."

Angie would eventually come around. All he had to do was work on Laura, and trust that God would take care of the rest.

Chapter Fifteen

A phone rang with an irritating jingle that cut through her brain. Laura opened her eyes and picked up her cell sitting on the table next to the bed. "Hello?"

"I'm sorry about last night."

Jack.

"What time is it?"

"Almost eight o'clock."

She flopped back against her pillows. "Why are you calling me this early?"

"Because I can't stop thinking about you." His voice was low, just above a whisper.

She closed her eyes. "Jack—"

He cut her off. "Besides, you promised to go to church."

"I can't."

"Why?"

"Think of Angie."

"I talked to her. Look, this is my fault. I wasn't listening when she said the youth group was going to the movies and I never gave her a heads-up about us going out."

Laura kneaded the bridge of her nose. No wonder Angie had been so upset. "You're an idiot."

"I know."

She smiled at his sheepish tone.

"Come to church with me. See what it's about, what I mean by trusting God, okay?"

She'd stayed in order to attend church with Jack. And she couldn't leave without facing Angie. "What time?"

"We need to leave by nine forty-five."

She heard Harry yip in the background.

Jack let out an annoyed sigh. "Hang on, I've got to let the dog out before he wakes up Ange."

Her heart froze. The more she struggled against the pull of her feelings for Jack, the deeper she sank. Kind of like quick-sand—more pleasant but just as scary.

"He takes forever to do his business," Jack said with a chuckle. She heard him whistle.

"Jack?"

"Yeah?"

Laura was used to facing down the toughest clients hag-gling over pricing. Attending church with a sweet thirteen-year-old girl, who might very well be mad at her, intimidated Laura more than the fiercest business owner. "What should I wear?"

"Jeans, a dress, whatever. It's casual."

She stared up at the canopy top of her old bed. Despite the pause of silence, she didn't want to hang up. Apparently Jack didn't, either. Finally, she whispered, "Thanks for taking me to the movies."

"Get used to it. I'm going to ask you out again, you know."

Her heart swelled at the warmth in his voice. "See you in a bit, then."

She clicked shut her phone and threw back the covers. She was going to church.

"Mom, let Jack help you into the truck." Laura stepped off the porch as Jack gave her mother his arm. Angie leaned against the SUV.

Squaring her shoulders, Laura marched toward her. "Angie, I'm sorry about the movies last night."

Angie shrugged. "It's okay."

"No, it wasn't. I don't want to mess up you and me. I don't want to come between you and your dad, either." Laura waited for Angie to reject her. It didn't happen.

Angie gave her a quick nod. "Thanks."

Laura leaned against the truck, too. "Do you mind if my mom and I join you for church?"

"I don't mind."

Laura studied her. There wasn't a hint of resentment. "Was that blond guy next to you Melissa's brother?"

Angie actually blushed. "Yeah."

"What's his name?"

"Tim."

"He's pretty cute." Laura watched Angie closely.

More blushing. "Yeah."

Laura fought the urge to take Angie in her arms. The girl's awkward responses confirmed it was her first crush. And Laura was privy to it. She remembered those days, the sweet innocence of noticing boys. But Laura had been too nervous and afraid to actually do anything about her crushes.

And here she was, years later with the same issues.

Jack climbed into the front seat. "Ready?"

"We are." Laura quickly slipped in the back next to Angie.

She caught Jack's gaze in the rearview mirror. The intensity she read in his eyes made her pulse race. Again, they felt like a family. An intense sense of belonging washed over her. Did Jack feel it, too?

At church, Laura grabbed her mother's hand after Jack helped her out of the SUV. "Here, Mom, walk with me."

"A pretty little church. I think they have a new minister. He's young," her mom said.

Jack slipped his hands in his pockets and slowed his steps to their pace. "Nice guy. He and his wife just had a baby."

What would that be like? Having a baby of her very own. Her insides softened and Laura glanced at Jack. What was wrong with her?

They entered the church and Jack introduced them to several people before taking a seat in the fourth row. Her mother settled in by an older lady and the two chatted easily.

Jack moved in next to her. "You're fidgety."

Laura stopped twisting her purse strap, and set it on the floor. "It's been awhile."

"I think you'll like it," he said.

"I hope so." For his sake, she'd keep an open mind.

The music started and everyone stood. Laura did, too. She spotted Angie with Melissa's family. Tim didn't look like he noticed Angie was there. He craned his neck to keep tabs on a little redhead two rows up. Poor Angie.

An ensemble of musicians who looked more like what you'd expect from a folk band played an upbeat song that clipped along faster than anything Laura had ever heard in church before. In no time, she found herself singing the simple chorus and clapping along.

The service went on that way—a couple cheerful songs and then some slower hymns. Everyone sang with passion. She could feel their exuberance resonating deep inside. A novel experience for church. She looked around. Many had their eyes closed, and a couple people lifted their hands toward the rafters. An odd exercise of surrender, but seeing them tugged at her heart. There was something beautiful going on here. Something pure.

The band changed tempo into a new song. The words were familiar to the hymn of "Amazing Grace," but the chorus was completely different. And haunting. Her throat tightened as she heard the words. She sang them in a ragged whisper.

…I once was lost, but now I'm found…

She glanced at Jack who had his head tilted toward heaven with his eyes closed. His voice rang out deep and lush. He really loved God.

And then Laura lost it. Tears streamed down her face and her lips trembled. She bowed her head, hoping to hide. The beauty of the song, the voices of Jack, men, women and children alike combined into a prayer of sorts. It was deafening and heartwrenching. And beckoning her to surrender.

Laura couldn't take it.

She slipped out of her seat and headed for the ladies' bathroom. Pushing open the door, she nearly collapsed with relief when no one was inside. She couldn't face a well-meaning stranger. Slipping onto a gold vinyl couch against the wall, she buried her face in her hands and wept.

Keeping her eyes closed, Laura couldn't deny the tugging at her heart. Jack's invitation to ask God into her life whispered through her mind. Was she ready to trust God?

She wanted to. She had to.

"God," she whispered, "I'm sorry for so many things, forgive me."

Could she do this by herself? In a ladies' restroom? Would God mind? She remembered the natural, practical way Jack approached prayer and knew it'd be all right. Jack had told her God loved her for who she was, where she was.

"And I want You in my life," she breathed.

She waited quietly, wondering if she'd feel different. Wondering if internal fireworks might go off. Instead, she felt like she'd made a sound decision. The right choice. Peace.

She felt a soft touch on her shoulder that made her jump. She hadn't heard anyone come in.

"Laura, are you okay?"

Angie.

Laura sniffed and lifted her head. "Yeah."

"What's wrong?"

"Nothing, nothing at all. I know God's real. I felt Him." Laura pointed to her chest. "In here."

Angie handed her a box of tissues.

"Thanks." Laura blew her nose and laughed. "Pretty weird, huh?"

"I don't think so. I know what you mean."

Laura could have shouted for joy. Angie wasn't giving up on God. Maybe they could learn to trust God together. If she'd still accept her friendship. "Did your dad send you in?"

Angie shook her head. "I saw you leave and wanted to make sure you were okay."

"Thanks." Laura draped her arm around Angie's back and gave her a squeeze. But Angie turned it into a full-fledged hug.

Laura almost started bawling again. She pulled back and smiled. Angie did, too.

"Come on, let's get back to church," Laura said.

Laura slipped into her row and sat down next to Jack.

He took her hand and whispered, "You okay?"

She squeezed and didn't let go. "Perfect."

Laura had heard beautiful music before, but today was different. God had shown up and taken residence inside her heart. The subtle differences unfurled. She wasn't the same. She felt new.

Jack didn't want to linger after church. He wanted to celebrate. Laura had made the decision to trust God with her life. She'd been so excited when she told him, that he'd almost blurted out his love for her right there in the pew. Instead, he introduced her to the pastor and the three of them had prayed together.

When they finally made it to the parking lot, Angie rushed toward them with her friend in tow. "Dad, can I go to Melissa's house? Her mom will bring me home."

Jack searched out Melissa's mom who nodded in agreement. "You better tell Laura goodbye. She's leaving after lunch. She's got an interview for a promotion at work tomorrow."

Angie's eyes widened. "When are you coming back?"

"Hopefully, next weekend."

Angie hesitated, and then gave Laura a quick hug. "Bye."

"Have fun." Laura winked.

Angie flushed a deep red, then she took off with her friend, the two of them giggling.

"What was that all about?"

Laura merely smiled. "Nothing."

Jack watched Angie climb into the Johnston's SUV. Melissa's older brother got in after her, and Jack wondered if the skinny kid sporting a surfer look was the reason for his daughter's blushes. "Please, don't tell me she's looking at Melissa's brother."

Laura's gaze flew to his. "It's what girls do."

Jack groaned.

Laura's mom laughed. "Don't worry, Jack. Angie's a good girl."

So was her mother. Jack shook off the thought, but the curious look in his daughter's eyes wasn't easy to ignore.

Jack sat in front of his computer pouring over patient billing, when his cell phone rang. "Hello?"

"Hi, Jack. It's Laura."

He leaned back in his chair and soaked in the sound of her voice. "Hey."

"Thank you for the Bible, by the way."

He'd placed one on the passenger seat of her car the morning before church. "You're welcome. I thought it would come in handy."

"It's perfect. I've been reading it every day and things are making sense. I feel…I don't quite know how to explain it."

"Energized?" Growth came through the word of God.

"Yeah, and clearer somehow. How's Angie, and my mom?"

"Everyone's good. Your mom told off her home health aide the other day." Jack chuckled.

"Oh no, what happened?"

He needed to ease the sudden tension in her voice, the worry. "I guess the aide didn't want to go over the insurance claim with anyone but you and that ticked Anna off. Your mom fired off that some people had *important* jobs to do. I tried to step in, but you'll have to take a look when you come home. The aide wouldn't release info to me. Your mom's proud of you."

Silence.

"Laura, did you hear me?"

"We're talking about the same Anna Toivo, right?"

Jack laughed. "The same."

"Look, Jack, there might be a problem with me coming home this weekend."

He braced for the worst. "Is everything okay?"

"Everything's fine. I've got this client retreat to attend, but then corporate wants me back in St. Louis for a couple days next week."

He closed his eyes. "You got the promotion."

"I don't know yet. But being called back is a good sign, don't you think?" Her excitement was palpable.

Anna had already hinted that she didn't expect Laura to come home. She said something always came up to keep her daughter away. A promotion would definitely impact Laura's time, keeping her away. From Angie. From him.

Jack sighed.

"Could you tell Mom for me? I'll call her later."

He didn't want it like this—her work before them. He'd been there, done that, only this time he was the one left waiting at home. He hated it. "Angie will be disappointed. She and Melissa made the junior high cheerleading squad and their first game is Friday night."

"I'm sorry. I'll make it up to her."

"What about me?" he said softly.

"I'll make it up to you, too." Her voice was light and cheerful. The excitement about her corporate opportunity rang through loud and clear.

He tried to match her tone. Now wasn't the time to get deep. "I'll hold you to that."

"I gotta go, Jack. My exit is coming up."

He wanted to say so much more, but not over the phone.

Jack stepped into Anna Toivo's kitchen. It smelled like melted margarine. She'd invited him and Angie over for dinner every night this week. He hadn't eaten this well since Joanne was alive. If he didn't watch it, he'd welcome Laura home with a spare tire around his middle.

"Angie is setting the table and you can make a salad," Anna said.

He made his way around the kitchen with ease, chopping garden greens. He made a small one because Laura wasn't there to enjoy it. He smiled. Her two favorite food groups were junk and lettuce.

"What's so funny?" Anna asked.

"I was just thinking about how much Laura loves salad."

"Rabbit food, if you ask me."

Jack laughed. He'd come to realize many things about Anna in Laura's absence. She was a stubborn lady with a ton of pride—the perfect combination to build a wall between mother and daughter. But she loved Laura.

And so did he.

When they sat down to eat, Jack prayed a simple prayer of thanks before ending with, "And keep Laura safe on the road. Amen."

Angie didn't miss a beat. "Did you talk to Laura?"

Jack passed the pot roast. "She might not be home this weekend."

"Why?" Angie whined.

Anna didn't look up. She plopped mashed potatoes on her plate and doused the whole thing in gravy. "Because Laura hides behind her job."

Angie looked at him, expecting him to say something.

"What?" Jack knew Laura was afraid, but things were bound to change. She said she was gaining clarity. But would that clarity lead to making room for them permanently?

"Can't you do something?"

"What do you want me to do, Ange? Give Laura some slack, she's been away from her work for weeks."

That didn't appease his daughter, or Anna.

"It's only a few more days," he said.

Anna remained quiet. So did Angie.

"I miss her, too." There, he'd said it.

"Did you tell *her* that?" Angie bullied him.

He narrowed his eyes but his daughter held his gaze without a waver. "Yes, Angie, I told her."

"What'd she say?" Angie was determined.

Jack's ears grew warm. "That she'd do the best she could."

"Maybe you should ask her out again, Dad. Someplace nice. Maybe that'd bring her home."

Jack looked at the expectant faces of his daughter and Anna. "Maybe, I will."

Later that night, after Angie had gone to bed, Jack dialed Laura's cell phone.

"Hello?" She sounded muddled, soft.

"Did I wake you?" He'd expected to get her voice mail, and leave a message.

"Jack? No. Well okay, maybe you did."

"I'm sorry."

"Is anything wrong?" Her voice hitched.

"No. It's not even ten o'clock there—shouldn't you be schmoozing at the retreat?"

"I didn't feel much like mingling."

He heard the smile in her voice. "Tired?"

"Hmm."

"Miss me?"

She laughed. "Is there a reason you called?"

"There is." He took a deep breath. Why was asking a woman out so hard? Even the second time. "Bring something nice to wear when you come home."

"Why?"

"Angie suggested that I ask you out for a real date. I think she feels bad about the movies. Anyway, I'd like to take you to dinner."

"Angie's idea, huh? How can I refuse?"

He smiled. "You can't."

"You're pretty sure of yourself, Dr. Stahl."

"A man can't have too many doubts."

But Jack had plenty. He just hoped their date would put them to rest.

Chapter Sixteen

Two nights later, Jack got a call from his sister in Lansing. It was about Angie. He wasn't in the mood to confront his daughter, but he wasn't about to let it go, either.

"Ange," he called. "Can you come down here, please?"

He heard sounds of a chair scraping against the floor.

"What's wrong?" She took the stairs slowly.

"That pajama party you went to in Lansing, why didn't you tell me boys were there?"

She paled.

"Why didn't you tell me?" His voice raised a notch.

Angie shrugged her shoulders. "Stacy's brother had a few friends over, it wasn't a big deal."

Jack nearly choked. He knew what fifteen-year-old boys were like. He'd been one. "No big deal? Then why did a girl have a hickey so big her mom saw it two weeks later? Explain the rules of that kissing game you played in the basement."

Angie's eyes widened, but she didn't utter a word.

"Lying is not an option, young lady."

"I didn't lie!"

Jack felt his patience slipping. "Not telling me is as good as lying. It's deceitful and I won't have it."

Angie's eyes flashed with defiance. "Like not telling me you were asking Laura out?"

"That's got nothing do with this."

"If I didn't see you at the movies, would you have told me you went out with her?"

Jack narrowed his eyes. She had a point, but he'd already come clean on that one. "This isn't about me. It's about you being alone with a boy. You're too young."

"I wasn't! I didn't even play their stupid game."

"How do I know, Ange?"

"Because I said so." Angie leaned against his computer desk with her arms folded.

"You purposefully didn't tell me the party plans before you went. You knew I wouldn't have let you go, isn't that right?"

She remained quiet.

"Where were Stacy's parents?"

"Upstairs."

Jack ran his hand through his hair. Angie's friend Stacy had always been involved when Angie got into trouble. He knew better than to let Angie go over there, but he'd caved in. He could kick himself now.

Maybe he needed to get tougher. If he didn't, things might get worse later. He looked at his daughter, wishing for the hundredth time for half the ability Joanne had in dealing with their daughter. Even more, he wished Laura were home.

"You're grounded for two weeks. No phone calls, no going over to Melissa's house. Straight home after school."

"But Dad—"

"I mean it, Angie. I don't know what I have to do to make you understand that I'm serious about lying."

"Aren't you going to even listen to my side?"

"I did. The matter's closed."

She huffed and puffed, then headed for the door. Harry trailing behind at her feet.

"Where are you going?"

"I'm going to take Harry outside." Her voice sounded thin and watery.

He let her go.

Laura passed the Welcome to Michigan sign and pressed the gas. At this rate, she'd make it to her mom's by eight-thirty. Saturday night, too. She'd made it home for the week-end, as promised.

Home.

She couldn't wait to pull in the drive and see two people who'd come to mean so much to her. She'd even missed her mother. Go figure. Coming home felt warm and comforting for the first time in ages. Something she'd always wished for. And now…

Laura checked the presents piled in the backseat that crinkled in the wind of her rolled-down window. A big glossy paged book about the history of the Upper Peninsula for Jack along with two pounds of gourmet coffee. A new marble rolling pin for her mom, a new outfit for Angie, a T-shirt for Ben and some dog toys for Harry.

She rubbed the back of her neck. After a week at work, her muscles felt tight. She'd left the retreat early, after Mr. Albertson was comfortable that A.L.I. would mesh well with his plant management. Cindy had gone with Laura, along with her sales manager, Jeff. It was during Friday night's cocktail party that Jeff had given her the news. Corporate was going to offer her the promotion to senior sales executive. She'd proved herself and everything had fallen into place.

Only something felt out of place inside.

This might be the only weekend she'd get home for a while. Her new position required more travel. Jack had asked her to dinner and that would be the perfect time to share her news. She ran her fingers through her hair. How would he respond?

She slowed as her mother's house came into view. Lights glimmered in the windows. The warm glow welcomed her.

The porch light flickered on and her mother peered out of the screen door. "Is that you, Laura?"

Harry scooted out past her mother's legs.

Laura laughed as Harry ran around her ankles, nipping at her feet. "Hey, little man, what are you doing in my mother's house?"

Angie joined her in the yard. "I'm glad you're here."

Laura opened her arms and Angie went into them like a long-lost friend, or maybe a little bit like a daughter might. She squeezed tighter.

"What is it?" Laura asked when she heard the girl sniff.

"My dad's being a jerk."

Laura's stomach fell. She didn't want to get in the middle of an argument. Would Jack be angry if she intervened? One look at the misery in Angie's eyes, and Laura knew she had to at least listen. "Help me with my bags and then tell me what happened."

Angie nodded.

Lugging her suitcase, Laura entered the kitchen followed by Angie and Harry. "Can you put those bags in the living room?"

Angie obeyed.

"And no peeking!" Laura gave her mom a quick hug. "So, what's going on?"

"She had a fight with her dad," her mom whispered.

"Do you know why?"

Her mom shrugged. "She's only been here a little while."

When Angie returned, Laura asked, "Does your dad know you're here?"

"Yeah."

Laura breathed easier, and glanced at her mom. "We'll be upstairs, unpacking."

Once seated on her canopy bed, Laura patted the spot next to her. Harry accepted the invitation and settled his head on Laura's knee. She looked at Angie. "What's up?"

Angie let out a frustrated groan and told Laura the whole story about the pajama party, finishing with Jack's accusations and grounding.

"Your dad's doing the best he can, Ange." She remembered the night Jack and Angie had stayed during the storm and the fears Jack had expressed about his kids. Her heart tightened. That night seemed so long ago.

Angie chewed her bottom lip. "But he wouldn't have let me go if he knew Stacy's brother had friends over, too. He's weird about that."

"You didn't give him a chance. He might have surprised you." Laura pushed a strand of Angie's hair away from her face. "Was the party fun?"

Angie shrugged.

Just then her mother hollered up the stairs that Jack was on the phone. She looked at Angie.

"Can you see if he'll change his mind about grounding me?"

Laura slid off the bed, leaving Harry to find a new spot. "I don't know, Angie."

"Please?"

Laura headed for the extension in her mother's old room, her gut churning. She was stepping right in between them. "Hello, Jack?"

"When did you get home?"

"About a half hour ago."

"I take it Angie's giving you the lowdown. I grounded her."

"I know." Laura sighed.

"You think I shouldn't have?"

"I didn't say that."

"But that's what you think."

"I don't know, Jack, two weeks is a long time when you're thirteen."

This time he sighed. "I know. Mind if I come over?"

"I was hoping you would. I've got a few things for you and Angie and my mom."

"Presents, huh?"

"Yup." She heard the smile in his voice and breathed easier. "I'll be right there."

When Laura returned to her room, Angie looked up. "Was he mad?"

"No."

"Will you talk to him? Melissa's having a cheerleading get-together next weekend and I really want to go."

Laura rubbed her forehead. "He's your dad, Ange. It's up to him. He's on his way over. Let's go downstairs and do presents."

Angie made an irritated sound, but she followed Laura down the stairs. Harry trailed after them.

Laura's heart flipped over when Jack stepped through the archway into her mother's living room. She'd been away only a week, but it felt longer. Missing him had been stronger, too.

His gaze caressed her. "Hi."

Without looking away, she held out a gift bag and forced her voice to remain steady. "This is for you."

Jack accepted the bag with a smile, but a quick glance toward his daughter revealed his tension.

Angie wouldn't look at him.

Laura remembered being in Angie's spot as a teenager. Back then, Laura's mother gave her the silent treatment and Laura hated it. But it was Angie wearing the chip on her shoulder. If only she could get Jack to see where his daughter was coming from. Get them to talk. It was worth a try.

Jack flipped through the pages of the book. "Thank you. This is perfect."

"You're welcome." Laura turned to watch Angie open her gift.

"I'll wear it to church tomorrow." Angie held the dark plum pantsuit against her. A chorus of admiration rang out, even from Jack.

After Laura's mom opened her rolling pin, Jack rose to leave. "It's late. We better go. Call me in the morning if you ladies would like go to church with us."

"We will, Jack. Good night. I'm going to bed, Laura," her mother said.

Laura nodded and followed Jack onto the porch, trying to ignore the obvious pointed looks coming from Angie.

"Ange, go on home, I need to talk to Laura a minute," Jack said.

The girl smiled as if knowing with Laura as her negotiator, she'd get her way. She took off running with Harry yipping along beside her.

After Angie made it into the barn, Jack sat on the porch swing. "Tell me why you think I'm being too harsh."

Laura sat next to him, contemplating how to get Jack to meet his daughter somewhere in the middle. He'd once asked for her help, she wasn't about to back off now. Not when she understood where Angie was coming from. "Didn't you play spin the bottle at her age?"

Jack looked horrified. "Did she tell you that one of the girls had a golf-ball-sized hickey two weeks later? These kids were going into a storage closet."

This was more serious than Angie had led on. "Angie said she didn't play the game."

"She's lied to me before."

Laura recognized the fear in Jack's eyes, the worry. This was bigger than one misguided pajama party. "Is there something else bothering you?"

His gaze pierced her. "I don't want Angie to end up like her mother."

"She's only thirteen!"

"But kids seem to know more these days, Laura. I took advantage of Joanne while she was under the influence and she paid dearly for it. We both did. I don't want Angie to end up in a premature marriage. I want her to go to college and fulfill her dreams."

"Have you talked to Angie about this, told her why you worry?"

He shook his head. "I don't want to tarnish her memory of her mom and me. I mean, we made it work, but it was no bed of roses. The kids were our common denominator, and our faith. We loved each other, but it was a quiet, dependable sort of thing. Not like what I feel for you."

Laura's heart dropped to the soles of her feet. She knew what he meant. Jack was in her thoughts more often than not. As much as she had cared for Anthony and thought she wanted to build a life with him, she'd never felt like this. The way she felt when she was with Jack. The way she felt *about* Jack.

His blue eyes searched hers. "Does that scare you?"

"Yes," she breathed.

He took her hand and twined his fingers with hers. "I know."

Laura stared at Jack's hand nestled around her own. A strong hand, capable, but gentle. The gold of his wedding ring gleamed in the porch light. She imagined Joanne's life with Jack had been full of exhilarating surprises, yet safe and secure. A kernel of envy pinched Laura's insides, like she'd stepped on a pebble in her shoe.

But this wasn't about them. This was about Angie.

They had the rest of the weekend to discuss their feelings and where they were headed. They had their dinner date.

She squeezed Jack's hand and let go. "I think you should be honest with Angie if you want her to be honest back. Tell her what you're really afraid of, Jack. Let her know how hard it was on you and Joanne. She might need to hear it."

"So, you don't think I should ground her?"

Laura shook her head. "I don't know. Given that she kept important information from you on purpose, maybe you should. But two whole weeks? Talk to her, then decide. Seems to me you already think it's too much or you wouldn't keep asking me."

He let out a sigh. "Maybe you're right."

Drawn by the warmth of him, Laura leaned her head on his shoulder. "Don't worry, you'll figure it out."

He slipped his arms around her. "I'm glad you're home."

"Me, too."

Chapter Seventeen

"**D**o you know where your dad is taking me?" Laura asked.

"Nope." Angie and Melissa both lay upon Laura's canopy bed, their chins resting in their hands. Harry sat next to them.

"Your hair looks awesome," Melissa said.

Laura looked in the mirror as she slipped a pair of pearl earrings in place. Her hair had been swept into a twist and she wore a little black dress. "Not even a clue?"

Angie laughed. "Even if I did, I wouldn't tell."

Laura caught Angie's gaze in the mirror. "Surprise, huh?"

The girl just grinned.

Laura twirled around. "How's this?"

"You look like a model," Melissa said in awe.

"Thanks." Laura slipped into a pair of high-heeled sling backs and then checked her watch. Another fifteen minutes before Jack came to get her. She took a deep breath. She didn't expect to feel this jittery. It was just dinner.

She made it down the stairs without mishap. Angie and Melissa were close behind.

In the living room, Laura's mother looked up from her weather forecast and grinned. "I have just the thing for you to wear."

"Oh?" Laura hoped it wasn't something gaudy. She waited

in the kitchen, her gaze fixed on the door while her mom dug around in her room. The girls slipped a bag of popcorn into the microwave. In no time the kitchen smelled like a movie concession stand, but Laura's mouth didn't water. Her nerves were so tight, her throat felt like parchment paper.

"Here." Laura's mom held out a delicate string of matched pearls. "Your father bought me these. They'll go with your earrings."

The wistful sadness in her mother's eyes took Laura's breath away, making the night seem that much more important. Special. Scary. She kicked off her shoes and turned around. "Could you put them on me?"

It took her mom a few shaking tries before she managed the clasp. She gave Laura's shoulders a squeeze. "Now turn around. You look so beautiful. Jack's going to think so, too."

Laura ran her fingers along the necklace. "Thanks, Mom."

"He cares about you, Laura. Deeply."

Laura glanced at Angie who channel surfed in the living room with Melissa. "Shhhh. Angie's in the next room."

Her mother waved her concern away with a click of her tongue. "As if she doesn't already know and is glad for it. I didn't like Anthony. I knew he wasn't the right man for you."

Laura looked into her mother's earnest eyes.

"But I sure like Jack."

Jack had showered and shaved, nicking his chin in the process. He wanted everything to be perfect tonight. He checked his watch, almost six-thirty. Time to go.

Grabbing his wallet and keys from his bedside table, he picked up his picture of Joanne. Running his finger across the glass, Jack was reminded how much Angie looked like her mother.

He'd followed Laura's advice. Last night he'd had the most amazing and uncomfortable conversation with Angie. But it was worth it, even if Angie's last words were "Does this mean I'm still grounded?"

He hoped he'd made Joanne proud, taking the lead in a discussion better suited for mothers and daughters. But Jack had put a guy's perspective on the whole thing. He knew he'd rattled Angie. Maybe even shocked her. At least she understood why he worried, and why he'd do his best to protect her.

Their relationship was not only healing, but also stronger. Much was due to Laura's influence and empathy. God had worked a miracle in their move north. Jack was grateful for connecting with his daughter. So much had happened in a short amount of time, but they'd grown as a family. A family about to grow by one more.

Jack was ready to be honest with Laura.

Staring at the photograph of his late wife, he whispered, "You'd like her, Jo. She's good with Angie. And with me." Then he slipped his wedding ring off and set it down beside the frame. And he headed out the door.

Jack knocked before stepping inside Anna's kitchen. Laura leaned against the kitchen table as she slipped into high heels. The dress she wore made his breath catch. Black silk hugged her slender form. "Are you ready?"

Her eyes widened with appreciation. "You look handsome."

Jack thought she might like his navy suit. It was the only reason he wore it. "You look beautiful."

The color in her cheeks deepened as she reached for her purse.

Jack held Laura's coat open for her, and glanced at his daughter. "Angie, listen to Anna. You've got our cell numbers if you need anything."

"They'll be fine. You two have fun." Anna winked at them.

Angie and Melissa were all grins and silly giggles.

Once outside, Jack offered Laura his arm. "Those shoes look dangerous."

She laughed. "They're higher than I normally wear."

He opened the passenger side door for her and whispered close to her ear, "I like them."

Laura slipped into the seat. "Where are we going?"

"You'll see."

They drove halfway to Houghton before pulling into a rambling Victorian inn that Anna said had wonderful food. It was the type of place for celebrations and cozy dinners. The dining room was lit only by candlelight. Just the kind of atmosphere he wanted.

Once seated and their orders given to their waitress, Jack noticed that Laura fiddled with her water goblet. She seemed nervous. Her attention strayed to the dance floor where a soft jazz band played. Several couples swirled to the music.

"Would you like to dance?" he asked.

"I would."

Maybe that would get them talking.

Jack's hand slipped to the small of her back. He'd missed her this past week. Pulling her close, he whispered, "Did I tell you how incredible you are?"

"Every time you look at me." She smiled.

Warmth spread through him. It showed. He rested his chin against her temple and whirled her around the floor.

"You're a good dancer," Laura said.

He eased her into a spin. "Joanne coaxed me into a ballroom class, since we attended a lot of fund-raisers."

As the tempo of the song slowed, their steps shifted into languid movements. Jack wished time could stand still. Satisfied just to hold her, he moved with the music. He'd never listened to jazz, but the bluesy sound confirmed what Jack wanted. He'd buy a whole shelf full of the stuff if he could dance with Laura the rest of his life.

When the notes of the last song faded into silence, Jack kissed Laura's forehead. She didn't stir. "You're not asleep, are you?"

She moved closer. "No."

"Our food's here."

"Hmm, I guess we'd better enjoy it, then."

Jack was just as hesitant to leave the dance floor. Once seated, he grasped Laura's hands in his own and bowed his head. He prayed softly over their meal, and then added a silent plea for the courage to tell Laura what needed said.

"Jack?"

He read the excitement in her eyes. "What's up?"

"I got the promotion."

His appetite shriveled and died. "Wow. That's great. Tell me about it."

"I'm headed to corporate so they can officially offer me a senior sales executive position. This means going after larger clients with bigger contracts and better commissions."

He reached for her hand and squeezed. He wanted to be happy for her, but all he could see ahead was endless weeks of waiting for her to come home. "Congratulations. Will you have the same territory?"

Her joy slipped, and her smile faltered. He saw a shadow of doubt cloud her blue eyes and that gave him hope. "I'll cover a larger area and report to corporate in St. Louis. There's more travel involved."

He sipped his water. "So you won't be home much."

She threaded her fingers through his. "Probably not at first."

The waitress arrived to refill their water glasses.

Silently, they dug in.

Laura's gaze searched his face. "You don't sound excited for me."

He wasn't good at faking it. "Laura, we've known each other a short time, but I've seen how well you handle things, how hard you work. You've got integrity and grit. You deserve this promotion and for that, I'm proud."

She smiled. "But?"

"I'll miss you." That was only part of the truth. He didn't

think this promotion was right for her. But how could he say it in a way that wouldn't insult or offend her?

"You and Angie can visit me and I'll come home—"

"—when you can," he finished for her.

Their main course arrived.

She looked at her plate, moving a few vegetables around before shifting her focus back on him. "What are you trying to say, Jack?"

"I want to know what you want. For us, from me."

"For now, can't we just see where this goes?"

He leaned back. If he didn't lay it on the line, he'd lose her to the demands of this new sales position. He didn't want to be one more pressure point for her, begging her to come home and spend time with him. "I want more."

Laura set her fork aside and stared at him. Hard.

He wasn't in the mood to eat, either. "Want to get this wrapped up and go for a drive?"

"Yes."

Jack flagged down the waitress for to-go boxes and the check. He refused Laura's offer to pay. By the time the valet pulled up his truck and they climbed inside, Jack noticed Laura shiver.

"Cold?" he asked.

"Freezing."

"The heat will kick in a minute or two. Move closer."

She slipped over to the middle and buckled up. "Thank you for a lovely dinner."

He laughed then. "Looks like we'll have more than enough for a midnight snack."

"I'm sorry, Jack. Seems like our dates keep getting ruined somehow." She kicked off her shoes, and tucked her feet underneath her.

He slipped his arm around her and squeezed. "Don't be."

Heading home, the silence got to Jack. He pulled into a parking lot of an ice cream stand that had closed for the night.

Leaving the motor running to keep the inside of the truck warm, he turned toward her.

"Laura, this past week felt empty without you." He caressed her cheek. Her skin felt soft. "I missed you, too."

Leaning close, he kissed her, determined to show her what he felt. He wanted this woman in his life, but he'd settle for nothing less than forever.

Pulling back, he twirled a lock of her hair that he'd loosened from her pins. "I care for you so much, I want to spend time with you."

Her eyes widened and she sat straighter. "I feel the same, but right now we might have to work around the distance."

"I don't want a long-distance romance."

She pulled out of his arms. "That's not fair, Jack."

"I want to build something lasting, something permanent. We need time together to do that."

Her eyes looked wary, as if she knew where he was going, what he wanted to say. Her hand came up in warning. "Jack—"

He had to come clean. "I love you."

Laura's heart softened when she heard those precious words. But waves of worry soon invaded the safe haven of Jack's truck. Staring at Jack's left hand, where his wedding ring used to be, her stomach tightened. She knew what came next. "It's too soon."

"I don't think so."

Laura swallowed hard. "Maybe we should talk about this another time."

"Why?"

Laura's head spun. "Because I'm afraid of what I think you want. Please, please don't ask me to choose between you and my job."

Jack looked at her, through her, his eyes searching, pleading, and full of love. "No one can give everything they have to a career without something getting lost somewhere. I've been there. I missed so much of my kids' lives and I can't get that time back. I don't want to miss anything with you. I don't want my kids to, either."

She closed her eyes, wishing she could block out his tender voice. "You want me to walk away from something I've invested years working toward."

"I'm asking you to consider walking toward something else. Something that won't put a frown line between your eyes and the stress I know you carry between your shoulder blades. Help me build my practice. Be my partner, Laura, in business and in life. Marry me."

Her jaw dropped. "We can't just get married!"

"Why not?"

She held up her index finger. "For one thing we've only known each other for a month."

"Five weeks."

She couldn't think straight, not with him looking at her that way. "Jack—"

"Tell me you don't love me."

She threw her head back and stared at the roof of his SUV. The glow from the dashboard made the inside of the truck like a warm place in a dream. She thought she'd loved Anthony after dating him for three years. Could she love Jack after only a handful of weeks? "I don't know."

"Time is relative, Laura. We've spent nearly every day together. We have something real here, and strong. My daughter loves you. My son will, too. What are you afraid of?"

"You and Ben and Angie—that's a lot of responsibility."

His eyes softened. "You're great with Angie. She needs you. I don't want to raise her alone."

"So you want to marry me for your daughter?" She knew it was weak, but self-preservation skills were hard to drop. Deflecting his affection made it easier.

Jack groaned. "No. I want you for you. I need you in my life."

"What if I can't make you happy? Or Angie?"

Jack ran a hand through his hair, messing it up. "That's not your job. It's up to me and it's up to Angie to be happy."

Sweet words indeed. Could they be true? Or would he throw them in her face when she failed, like Anthony had? She couldn't make Brooke like her. In the end, Anthony had blamed her because she'd put her career first. But how could she not? Her job never let her down. It was the safest place she knew.

"Jack, can we just go home? Please?"

He sighed. "Okay, okay. I get it, you need to think it through."

The drive home was short and silent. Laura's head throbbed by the time they pulled into the drive and Jack turned off the engine.

Before they got out, Jack turned to her. "I know you've got issues with your mom. Things you haven't worked out. You and your mom may never be the way you want in this lifetime, but she needs you, too."

Laura's eyes welled with tears. Jack didn't understand what it felt like to never measure up, to never be enough. Could she be enough for him? And Angie? What if she failed them all?

He covered her hand with his. "Laura, it's time to let go and live."

She pulled her hand away and dashed at her tears. "I've tried but it still hurts—every time I come home."

"Of course it hurts. I'm not asking you to deny how you feel. Feel it fully then give it away. Give it to someone who can take it away."

That got her hackles up. "Who is that, Jack—you? Just let you love all my troubles with my mom away, is that what you're saying? And we'll all live happily ever after? Life's not like that."

"I know all about life." His voice hardened. "I also know that if you'd let God have your hurt, then maybe you'd take a chance on me. And Angie and Ben."

She stared at him. "How can you be so sure?"

"Because life's a risk you have to take. You can't spend it hiding. No matter how successful your career, is that the only legacy you want to leave behind?"

What he offered was not something she could control. She'd have to trust him, and God to make it work. Relying on others wasn't one of her strengths.

"Come on, baby doll, take the risk."

His gaze bore into hers as she battled with her desire to say yes. "I can't."

She'd already failed him. She slipped out of the passenger side door and her heels sank into the dewy grass. The night's chill seeped into her blood. Laura had never felt so cold.

Jack met her at the front of the truck and gripped her arms. "Laura, don't do this. Don't run away."

"I'm not. I just need to think. Give me some space." There was always a price to pay for success. Sacrifice. She knew that. But what was she willing to sacrifice this time?

Laura unclenched her hands, but she didn't touch him. She didn't want to cling. That'd only make this worse.

"I love you, Laura. And I'm not going anywhere. You can have your time, but make the right choice." He gently touched his lips to hers.

She tasted her tears as they mixed into Jack's sweet kiss. Before she could respond he pulled back and walked away, toward the barn and his apartment.

The next morning, Jack stepped outside after seeing Angie off to school. He noticed Laura's light blue convertible had its trunk open. He walked toward the house.

He saw Laura step onto the porch. She wore a thick cotton sweater and jeans with sneakers. No matter what she wore, he thought she was beautiful. His heart flipped in his chest, only this time it made him feel sick. Homesick for her.

"Hi," she said.

"You were going to say goodbye, I hope."

She took a step down from the porch. "After I was packed."

He looked in the trunk, and his heart sank. "You've got a lot of luggage in there. How come?"

She buried her hands in her back pockets. "I don't know when I'll be back."

That stung. He wanted her to love him. He stood on the grass, below her. "This isn't a decision of the mind, you know."

"We're not impulsive kids. I'm not impulsive at all."

Once his mind was made up, he rarely second-guessed his decisions. Letting Laura go didn't feel right. It scared him. He didn't feel as confident about her coming around as he had last night. He'd laid awake too long letting the doubts creep in. Just like they did now, seeing all that luggage.

"Jack?"

"What should I tell Angie?" His gut twisted when he saw tears well up in her eyes.

"Tell her I'm sorry I missed her this morning. Tell her goodbye for me."

It sounded so final.

She stepped down a step. "I'm sorry, Jack."

He brushed his hands up her arms, and pulled her into an embrace. He felt her shudder. "Don't."

"I've got to go." She held on briefly then pulled back with a sniff. Wiping her eyes, she gave him a watery smile. Then she turned to wave at her mom who stood in the doorway looking grim.

Jack let her go. He had to. There was nothing more he could do, but pray and trust God would bring her back.

Chapter Eighteen

Laura threw her keys on the kitchen table of the hotel suite in St. Louis. Cold silence greeted her, nothing more. She was alone in every sense of the word. A safe place to be once upon a time, but now it felt hollow compared to what she'd left behind.

She made her way to the fridge for a Diet Coke. Popping the top, she collapsed onto a leather sofa and took a long drink. A half-empty bag of Oreo's sat on the coffee table. She'd never look at those cookies without thinking of Jack.

It had been two days since she'd left. Corporate had filled her time reviewing client lists, strategic calling plans and making the rounds of headquarters. Seeing Anthony happy and in love was hard to take, considering her own love life.

Jack lurked in her dreams at night and stole away her concentration during the day. She broke into the Oreo's with a satisfying tear just as her cell phone rang.

"Hello?"

"Hi, Laura, it's Angie."

She took a calming breath. "Is everything okay?"

"Yeah, I was just wondering if you were coming home this weekend."

If Jack had put his daughter up to calling, it was a low blow. "Where are you?"

"At your mom's."

Laura swallowed her irritation. "Did your dad ask you to call?"

Silence.

"Ange?"

"He told me not to. Please don't tell him."

Laura closed her eyes.

"So are you coming home?"

"I don't think so." Laura heard a muffled scraping sound coming through her phone.

"She said she's not sure." Angie's voice sounded far away.

"Ange? Did my mother ask you to call me?"

More shuffling. "No. I asked her if I could use her phone to call you. I didn't want my dad to overhear. Are you mad?"

"No, I'm not mad. Is my mom standing right there?"

"Yeah."

Memories of her mom nosing in on every call Laura had ever gotten as a teenager blazed through her mind. It had bugged her then, but visualizing her mother doing the same to Angie made her smile. "Can you do me a favor? Walk out to the porch, okay?"

Angie giggled. "Okay."

Laura heard the screen door slam through the phone. She'd always loved the sound of that screen door. Can a heart shrivel up and die?

After an awkward silence, Angie asked, "Did you and my dad have a fight?"

Laura's eyes filled with tears. "No."

"Did you break up with him? He's been really quiet."

Laura swallowed hard. She'd hurt him. Jack Stahl was hurting just like her, all because of her fear. "Look, Ange, I'm confused about some things."

"About my dad?"

"Yes. I just…" Laura's voice wavered and broke. She

couldn't explain it to a thirteen-year-old kid when she didn't understand it herself.

Silence.

"I don't mind if you date my dad, Laura. I think you two make a good couple. For real."

Laura's gut twisted. "Thanks, hon. That means a lot."

"You're coming home sometime, though, right? You've got to come to a game. Melissa and I made first squad."

She smiled. "Of course I'll be back. I wouldn't miss you cheerleading. Can you e-mail me your schedule?"

"Sure. I, ah, I really miss you."

Nope, her heart hadn't died, because it ached. How'd this teenager burrowed her way in so deeply? "I miss you, too, but I'm just a phone call away."

"It's not the same."

"I know. I love you, Ange, I really do," Laura blurted. Admitting that released something inside, making her shoulders sag.

"I do, too. You, I mean."

Laura closed her eyes. "Can you put my mom on the phone?"

"Yup. Bye," Angie said.

Laura heard the screen door squeak open then slam shut again.

"Is that you, Laura?"

"Hey, Mom, how are you feeling?"

"A little tired, but I'm okay. I'm worried about you."

"Me?" She could picture her mother pursing her lips. She always knew when Laura wasn't telling the truth.

"Jack looks like he lost his best friend."

Laura rolled her eyes. "Mom, is Angie right there?"

"She's not blind, you know. Things happen for a reason, Laura. Interruptions in life can turn into treasures worth cherishing more than your dreams."

"Thanks, Mom." Jack and Angie were more than just interruptions in her life. And so was her mother. Maybe they were the treasures she needed to make new dreams.

* * *

The following Monday, Laura walked into her Wisconsin office bright and early. She'd spent a miserable weekend researching leads and working out at the gym. Laura slumped into her chair and flicked on her computer and scanned her e-mails.

Angie's name caught her eye. As promised, she'd e-mailed Laura her cheerleading schedule. As she scrolled down, an e-mail from Jack seized her attention.

Hey Laura,
Your mom's fine and feeding Ange and me like crazy. She's taken us under her wing. We miss you.
Jack.

Laura read the note again. Obviously, he didn't want to send something personal on Angie's e-mail. But Laura could read between the lines. He wanted her home.

Home.

Laura's eyes burned. She blinked a few times, but tears gathered anyway. Jack, Angie and her mother were her family, her real home and safe haven. She needed them. She'd asked God into her life, but maybe it was time she trusted Him to give her direction.

"Laura?" Her assistant stood behind her chair.

"Yeah."

"Who's Jack?"

Laura glanced down at the computer screen. She'd rested her fingertips on Jack's part of the e-mail. "The guy who lives next door to my mother."

Cindy smiled wide. "No wonder you want to go home on weekends."

"Yeah." Her heart tore in two.

"Are you in love with this guy?"

Laura felt a tear trip over her eyelid and roll down her cheek. "Yes."

"Then what are you doing *here* if he's *there?*" Cindy said.

Something deep inside Laura snapped. The answer was simple. She wanted new dreams, different dreams than her job could provide. "I honestly don't know."

Just then, the receptionist set an arrangement of twelve long-stemmed pink roses on Laura's desk. "These came for you."

Cindy grinned. "I bet I know who they're from."

The heady scent filled the air. With trembling fingers, Laura flipped open the envelope and read the card.

Come home,
Jack

She gripped the edge of her desk. If ever Laura needed proof of God's answer to her prayer, this was it.

After coming home from work, Jack sat at his kitchen table staring at the same Bible verse he'd been trying to read for the last half hour. He'd confirmed with the flower shop that his delivery had been made, but Laura hadn't called. That sent a pretty strong message. She chose her job. It was over.

The sound of Angie's frightened voice screaming his name jerked him out of his daze.

She tore through the door and threw herself into him. "Dad! There's something wrong with Anna."

Jack sprinted for the house, Angie trailing behind him. He flung open the door and ran into the kitchen. "Anna?"

Anna Toivo sat at the kitchen table dazed and glassy eyed. Her lips moved but no sound came out, no words. Harry lay at her feet, his brown eyes looking worried.

"Is she going to be okay?" Angie whimpered.

"Get a pillow and a blanket," Jack ordered as he grabbed the phone.

"What's wrong with her?"

"Just do it, Ange." Jack punched in 911. After giving the dispatcher the address and situation, he took the blanket from his daughter and covered Anna. He placed the pillow under her feet, and then sat next to her wrapping his arm around her shoulders to keep her in place. He didn't want her falling over before the paramedics arrived.

Angie's eyes shimmered with tears. "Will she be okay?"

"We've got to get her to the hospital," Jack said.

"Are you going to call Laura?" Angie whispered.

"I'll call her on the way. Do you want to go to Melissa's house?"

Angie shook her head. "I want to go with you."

Jack wasn't about to refuse. Anna had become part of their family and if something went wrong, he'd give Angie the chance to say goodbye. He didn't want her left behind. Not this time.

"Anna, can you hear me? The ambulance is on the way." He looked into the older woman's eyes. Her hands were cold.

She nodded.

Jack closed his eyes with relief. She was coherent. That had to be a good sign. He glanced back at Angie. "Now's a good time to pray."

Chapter Nineteen

"Hello?" Laura pressed her cell to her ear.

"It's Jack."

The dull scream of a siren in the background cut through her brain, sending a chill into her heart. "What's wrong?"

"You're mom's okay, but we're on the way to the hospital. She's had another stroke."

Laura clutched the steering wheel. *Oh God, no, no!*

"Laura?"

"I'm here." She swerved away from the center line when a truck blared its horn.

"Where are you?"

"I'm on route 26. I'll meet you at the hospital in about an hour."

"You're where?"

The confusion in his voice made her smile, but the situation made her sick with worry. "I got your roses, Jack. I'm coming home for good."

Silence.

Was he smiling? She imagined his face and the intensity of his blue eyes. She felt his presence through the phone. She couldn't speak. She didn't have to.

"Tell my mom to hang on, I'll be there soon," she finally said.

"I will. Drive safe."

She stepped on the gas with clenched teeth. The reality of her mom's life hanging in the balance washed over her with sickening speed. Second strokes weren't good. They were always more serious, even fatal.

Don't do this, God!

She drove faster, her car hugging the curves with ease. She barely noticed the blaze of fall color that brightened the farther north she drove. Racing to the hospital wasn't the homecoming she'd pictured—certainly not what she had planned, but she'd deal with it. No matter how bad her mom's stroke, they'd make it through this. They had to.

Laura glanced at the roses. They were a family now. Laura belonged to a real family. She was over being afraid of what that meant. It was time to step up. It was time to stop hiding her heart.

When she finally burst through the emergency entrance, Laura scanned the waiting area. Angie hung her head in her hands while Jack rubbed his daughter's back. Aunt Nelda paced the floor. All three of them looked up as Laura approached. Angie ran toward her.

"How is she?" Laura asked as she hugged Jack's daughter close.

"They're giving her a drug treatment to break up the clot. It's supposed to take awhile," Jack said.

Aunt Nelda squeezed Laura's shoulder. "If Jack and Angie hadn't been there… Your mom had the stroke in the ambulance, but they pulled into the hospital fifteen minutes later. That's a very good thing."

Laura kissed the top of Angie's head while she looked at Jack. "You were in the ambulance?"

Jack's eyes were red rimmed but steady, and comforting. "Angie, too. Anna wasn't alone. We held her hand the entire time."

Laura broke down with a sob, but managed to whisper, "Thank you, Ange, for being there for my mom."

Angie's shoulders shook, too. "I'm glad you're here."

Jack's arms came around them both. "We're all here for Anna. That's the important thing."

"How'd you get here so fast?" Aunt Nelda asked.

Without looking away from Jack, Laura said, "I was on my way home."

"It's a miracle you were so close," her aunt said.

"That and a dozen roses," Laura whispered. She breathed in Jack's scent, taking comfort from the strength of his embrace. She vowed she'd never leave him again.

He gathered Aunt Nelda into their circle. "Maybe we could say a prayer for Anna."

Laura nodded.

"Go ahead, Jack," Aunt Nelda whispered.

Laura's heart quickened as she felt Jack's prayer roll through her. But she prayed, too, hoping she could make a deal.

God? Please keep my mom from dying. Let me talk to her. If You'll do that for me, I'll let go of all the hurt I have and give it to You if You'll just give me one more chance.

Jack handed Laura a can of ginger ale. They'd been waiting an hour and still there'd been no word. He threaded his fingers through hers. Bringing her hand to his lips, he kissed her knuckles. "You're home."

She smiled, her eyes tearing up yet again. "This hospital certainly doesn't qualify."

He nodded. They weren't there yet, but they would be. He rubbed his thumb along the inside of her palm. They'd have a lot to talk about, plans to make, but that would have to wait in order to care for Anna.

He looked at Angie who leaned her head on Laura's shoulder. Poor kid. She'd taken this hard, but now that Laura had arrived, she'd calmed down. The fact that Angie turned to Laura for comfort gave Jack a sense of peace. Marriage was right for all of them. But when?

If it were up to him, he'd have the minister marry them this weekend. He leaned his head back and sighed. Laura wasn't ready for that. Until she was, he'd just have to wait.

They sat another half hour without word. This couldn't be good. Jack braced himself for bad news when a solemn-looking doctor stepped into the waiting area and asked for Laura.

Anna had been transferred to the ICU so they could keep a close watch on her overnight. The next twenty-four hours were critical. The doctor's warning was stern, only Laura and Nelda were allowed in, one at a time, for a few minutes each.

"You go on ahead, Laura. I'll talk to the doctor," Nelda said.

Laura turned to Jack. "You won't leave?"

"You're our ride home." He gave Laura what he hoped was an encouraging smile. She looked scared, which tore him up. All he could do was pray, but that didn't feel like enough.

"Is Anna going to die?" Angie whispered.

"I don't know, sweetheart. She's in God's hands. We all are."

Laura stepped into the ICU where the nurse directed her to her mother's bed in the corner. The whole thing reminded her of those medical shows on TV. Only this was real.

"Hi, Mom." She gently took her mom's hand. Her skin felt warm and alive.

"Is that you, Laura?" Her voice was weak and ragged. Her mother's eyes fluttered open. She looked the same, hardly any drooping, but she couldn't squeeze Laura's hand.

"Don't talk, Mom. Save your strength for when you come home, okay? I'm not leaving this time, and I can help you with your exercises," Laura rambled to keep from bawling.

Her mom's lips turned up slightly. "I'm sorry."

Tears rolled down Laura's cheeks. "I wanted to come home, Mom. Jack sent me these beautiful roses with a note telling me to come home. Wasn't that something? I was already on my way when he called from the ambulance."

"I've never been a good mother...."

Laura nearly choked. Either her mother couldn't hear her or she was saying goodbye. "No, Mom, don't talk, just rest. When you're better we can talk."

"It's not your fault...."

"Shh." Laura couldn't handle a before-I-die conversation. Somewhere in her racing mind, Laura thought if she didn't let her mother say the words, then her mother would grow stronger and live. Her mother had to live.

"I do love you, Laura." Her mother's voice was barely audible.

"I love you, too."

Her mom closed her eyes. The lines on her face eased and she looked peaceful.

Panic seared through Laura as she felt for her mother's pulse. She wilted when she found it beating strong. She rubbed her mother's hand. "Don't leave me, Mom. Not now. Not when I finally understand."

She laid her forehead against the back of her mom's hand and stayed that way. She didn't want it to end here. She needed more time. She hoped God gave her more.

"Go home, Jack. And take Laura with you. She's exhausted. Anna's still stable. Laura can come back tomorrow," Nelda said.

Jack agreed. He would have left a long time ago but Laura had wanted to stay and he couldn't refuse her. She'd fallen asleep in a chair. "Call me if anything changes."

Nelda gave him a quick hug. "I will."

Jack knelt in front of Laura. He brushed back a lock of wispy blond hair that had fallen across her forehead. "Laura."

She pulled his coat closer.

He jostled her shoulder. "Laura?"

Her eyes opened and she smiled.

His heart thumped. "Dreaming of me?"

"Wouldn't you like to know?"

"Come on, sleeping beauty, we'd better go home—your aunt's orders. Your mom's doing great. The nurses promised to call if anything changes. Besides, your aunt is staying the night."

Laura sat up and stretched. Her hair reacted to the static from his coat and stuck straight up in the air. Her eye makeup smeared further when she rubbed her eyes. She was a beautiful mess as she fumbled in her purse for keys.

"Let me drive."

She handed them over.

"Come on, Ange." Jack nudged his sleeping daughter curled up on the small couch.

As they reached Laura's car, Jack unlocked the passenger door and found a vase full of pink roses buckled in with care. He gently lifted the arrangement.

"You sent her flowers?" Angie asked with a broad grin. "Way to go, Dad."

He lifted the seat for his lanky daughter to climb into the back. "I see now that I'll have to buy flowers more often."

Jack shifted into gear and backed out. The trip home remained quiet. When he unlocked the door and pushed into the kitchen, Anna's walker stood near the fridge.

Laura froze.

"Angie, go get Harry and your pj's. I think you should stay the night over here."

Angie glanced at him then at Laura. "I'll be right back."

Jack waited until he heard the door shut, before he took the vase out of Laura's hands and set it on the kitchen table. Then he pulled her into his arms. "Your mom's going to be okay, Laura. You can relax. The doctor said it could have been much worse."

"I'm so grateful you were here. I never should have left. What if—"

He kissed her nose. "Hush. You're here now. Forget about the what-ifs, okay?"

She nestled close against him and nodded.

Jack pulled back when he heard Angie's footsteps on the porch. "I'm going to tuck Angie into bed. Will you be okay for a minute?"

"Yes, go ahead." Laura reached into the fridge for a can of diet pop, and then she wandered into the living room.

Angie entered the kitchen with her overnight bag followed by a tail-wagging Harry.

"Come on, let's get you upstairs."

Jack knelt beside Angie's bed once she'd climbed in under the covers. Harry turned around at least three times before finally lying down next to her. He scratched the dog's ears, and looked at his daughter. "Are you okay?"

"Yeah."

He kissed her forehead. "I'm proud of you. You did exactly what you needed to do and that helped make all the difference for Anna."

"I was totally scared." Angie put her arm around Harry and cuddled him close.

"Me, too. Sleep tight." He stopped in the doorway. "I love you, Ange."

"I love you, too, Dad."

He closed the door. The last two years had been difficult but he'd made it through that dark tunnel and his kids had come along with him. Maybe at different intervals of growth, but neither one remained in the dark.

He walked into the living room and spotted Laura sprawled on the couch under a throw blanket. Her eyes were closed. He watched her, loving the way the she looked even in sleep. He'd found his soul mate when he'd least expected it and God's timing was right. Perfect. He was more than ready.

"Don't go yet," Laura yawned.

"It's late."

"Please?" She scooted up to make room for him.

He sat down and rubbed the back of her neck with his fingers.

"Jack, I don't know where to start," she said.

"You don't have to. We can talk tomorrow." He brought her hands to his lips and kissed the third finger of her left hand. "This won't be empty for long."

"I'm still scared," she said.

"I know."

She pulled free and gestured in a sweeping motion. "You and me living here with my mom. We'll have to live here you know. We can't start out in that little apartment."

"I know, but we can build a house on the edge of those woods. It'll take time."

She smiled. "Do you also know that I love you?"

His heart beat faster. "I was hoping you did."

"But I'd like some time to get used to all this."

"It's your timetable, baby doll, just don't take too long." He'd accept that she loved him and be satisfied. For now.

She leaned toward him. "I promise I won't. Do you mind if I kiss you?"

He met her halfway, cradling her face. "I was hoping you would."

Their lips touched and he savored the sweetness. It wasn't going to be easy, but he'd tell Laura how important it was to get it right this time. He wanted to face his kids on his wedding day with a clear conscience. He'd need her help.

She tucked her head on his shoulder. "I'm not used to feeling like this. My future's wide open. It's frightening."

He kissed her forehead. "I'll be with you, every step of the way. We'll be fine as long as we keep God first."

She nodded.

"I better go so you can get some sleep."

"Jack?"

He turned. "Yeah?"

"Thank you for my roses."

"You're welcome." As he watched her eyes close, Jack whispered a prayer of gratitude for all he'd been given.

Chapter Twenty

Humming under her breath, Laura walked into ICU. Jack had tucked a warm quilt over her before he'd left. She'd never felt more cherished.

He'd even driven her to the hospital this morning and promised to call when he'd finished with patient appointments. As long as the station nurse cooperated, together they'd tell her mother about their plans.

Anna Toivo's prognosis was good. They'd keep a close eye on her the next few days, but otherwise she was in good shape. Even her blood pressure had stabilized within normal range. The only bad news was that her mom might not regain the use of her left side. Only time and therapy would tell. Laura humbly thanked God for the miracle of her mother's life.

Sitting in the tiny chair next to her mother's bed, Laura whispered, "Hi, Mom."

Her mother's eyes opened and brightened with recognition. "Hi, Laura."

"How are you feeling?"

"I can't move my leg or my arm and my hand feels tingly, but I'm better than I was yesterday."

Laura smiled. Her mother sounded stronger than she'd ever

heard her. "You'll need physical therapy, but I'll take you for as long as needed. Your speech is good. Does it hurt to talk?"

"No."

Laura shifted in her seat. "Good, because I have to ask you about something that you said last night. Are you up to it?"

Her mom's blue eyes narrowed. "Go ahead."

Laura licked her lips. "You said it wasn't my fault. What's not my fault, Mom?"

Her mother sighed. "Oh, Laura, I wasted so much time. You were the prettiest little baby, but I was scared to death of you. I felt so awkward, but your father took to you as naturally as, well a parent should. I never shook those feelings, no matter how hard I tried to be a good mother. When your father died, I didn't begin to know how to help you through it. I couldn't even help myself. It was the lowest point of my life."

Laura squeezed her mother's hand. Her mother had been devastated and isolated in her grief. It was all she could do to get out of bed. "I couldn't do anything right, could I?"

"It wasn't you, Laura. It was me. Your father and I knew each other for years, but we married late in life. I didn't plan on having babies. I honestly didn't think it possible at my age. I was content to be married and keep my job."

Laura's breath caught. "I didn't know that you worked outside of the house."

"I managed a bank in Houghton for years."

"Why didn't you ever tell me?"

"Because I gave it up before you were born. I promised to stay home, which pleased your father. But I regretted making that promise, especially after your dad was gone."

Laura looked at her mother with new respect and understanding. She'd given up her source of pride for her. "Why didn't you go back after Dad died?"

Her mother shrugged. "I should have but so much had changed by then. I made too many excuses. After being a homemaker for twelve years, I only saw the reasons why I couldn't go back to work. I was afraid, plain and simple. I took it out on you and that wasn't fair."

"I'm sorry." She understood her mother's resentment. Her mother had a family—a daughter who would have supported her, but her mom had given up.

The entire time Laura had been away, she worried about resenting Jack for asking her to choose him her job. But she realized it was her choice, the right choice, to come home.

Laura chose family.

What she'd learned at her job would only help her build a new career with Jack. If that wasn't enough, Laura had options in Houghton, perhaps the college. She'd find her niche, and flourish knowing she had loving support at home. She didn't have to hide anymore. She didn't want to.

"It's not your fault that I envied you for having the courage to go away to college. You did so well, getting promoted and traveling. I gave up driving because I was afraid of hitting another deer. And there you were, driving everywhere. I felt like a failure."

Laura squeezed her mother's hand. Why did it take so long for her mother to tell her all this? "You're not a failure, Mom."

Her mother's eyes misted over. "I felt sorry for myself because of the choices I made. I hid behind the promise I made to your father. Making no moves was easier than venturing into unknown territory. I see so much of me in you, Laura. You've been hiding behind your job. Afraid of letting yourself love Jack. Partially because of that Anthony fella, but I helped make your insecurities, too. I'll never forgive myself for that."

Tears ran down Laura's cheeks. "You have to, Mom."

"Why?"

"Because I forgive you. Because God forgave me. Because we can be whole now."

"Oh, Laura." Her mother reached out her good arm. "I'm so

very proud of you, but I see my own stubbornness in you. A career is a good thing, but it's not the only thing. Family is more important. Family lasts forever."

"I know that now." Laura embraced her mother, and they stayed locked that way until the balled up hurt was finally unraveled and released.

After getting permission from the ICU nurse and promising not to stay more than a few minutes, Jack stepped through the swinging double doors. He spotted Laura immediately.

She turned as if sensing him, and smiled.

Wrapping his arm around her waist, he kissed her hair. "Hi."

"Hi," she whispered.

"How are you, Anna?" Jack said.

Anna's brow furrowed, but her eyes twinkled. "When are you going to marry my daughter?"

"Mom!" Laura buried her head into his shoulder.

Jack laughed. "Soon, Anna. Hopefully, very soon. With your permission."

Anna's smile was quick and bright. "Of course you have it. Now, I'd like to offer you an early wedding present."

Jack looked at Laura, who shrugged. "What's that?"

Anna reached out her good hand.

He and Laura both took it.

"I want you to have the house," Anna said.

"Mom—" Laura's voice was full of awe.

"It's yours to make over as you see fit, but promise me you won't ever sell it. It has to stay in the family and go to your children and then their children."

Jack glanced at Laura. He hadn't thought about having more kids, but he wanted them with her. Definitely a topic they'd have to discuss. "What do you think?"

Her beautiful, blue eyes shimmered. "I love that house."

He hugged her close. "Me, too."

* * *

Later that night after dinner, after they'd told Ben and Angie about their engagement, Laura followed Jack outside and watched Harry scamper into the tall grass. The sun hung low in the sky and a cold wind blew in from Lake Superior. She shivered.

Jack wrapped his arm around her as they walked. "Penny for your thoughts?"

"I think it's going to be an incredible sunset," she said.

"Looks like raspberry-colored ribbons."

Laura snuggled closer. "My dad used to say something like that. All those years ago when I'd sit and watch the sun go down, I couldn't wait to leave this place. And now, here I am, hoping I never have to leave again. So much has changed."

"Everything's changed for me." Jack pulled her close. "I met the woman of my dreams and I'm going to marry her."

"You're getting an old house that needs renovating, an unemployed bride and her ailing mother. I sure hope I don't become your nightmare."

"Not a chance. You're my business partner for as long as you want the position. As for my life partner, when do you want to start?"

Laura felt more than just protected. She could share her fears and dreams with a man who not only understood her, but loved her anyway. "I love you, Jack. I want to start our life, and make new dreams, and build your vet practice and all the things you offered. Why endure a long engagement?"

"My thoughts exactly."

She smiled. "I was thinking that maybe New Year's Eve might be nice for a wedding."

"Very nice." He kissed the corner of her mouth.

Laura cradled his face with both hands and kissed him. It was then she knew souls could touch. Jack was her soul mate. New Year's Eve seemed both like a long time and the perfect time to get married.

She tipped her head back. "We're going to be a real family, aren't we?"

"A happy one, I think."

Laura peeked at the house where she grew up. Those two windows that had always reminded her of a pair of eyes glowed from the lights that had been left on. A shade hung halfway down one of the windows. It looked like the house was winking—glad to have a happy family within its walls once again.

Epilogue

"What do you think, Mom? Throw the bouquet now?" Laura's fingers tightened around her mixed bundle of pink roses and evergreens.

"You're rushing it, Laura. Let people eat their cake first. You can do that before you go." Her mother's eyes crinkled with amusement. "Are you in a hurry to leave your own reception?"

"No," Laura answered quickly, her cheeks blazing.

Her mother patted her hand. "I don't blame you a bit."

Laura watched Jack twirl Angie around the dance floor, and her heart swelled. Angie had been thrilled to pick out her dusty-pink bridesmaid gown. She'd helped Laura choose the guys' ties, too. Both Jack and Ben had been appalled to wear what they referred to as an offensive color, but eventually they accepted dark pink.

Jack and Laura had booked the inn where they'd had dinner the night he'd proposed. They had reserved the rooms and the restaurant for the night. The same jazz band had been available, so they snatched them up as well.

"Laura, here's Ben. You two go join Jack and Angie. I want to take a picture." Aunt Nelda herded them along.

"Hey, I missed you," Jack whispered when Laura grabbed hold of his hand.

"Come on, more photos." Laura looped her arm through Jack's and grinned. She'd only been away from him a few minutes, but tonight was special. They didn't stray far from each other.

Ben and Angie stood like bookends on either side of them, while her aunt's camera flashed. At least ten people gathered to take pictures of their own. Nancy was one, and Laura's former assistant Cindy was another. Jack's parents joined in too, their digital camera clicking away.

Laura absorbed the laughter and love surrounding them, feeling blessed. She'd never forget this night. She looked forward to building a lifetime of memories with her family and Jack's. A blended family she hoped to one day expand, with her husband's help.

The grandfather clock began to chime announcing the approaching midnight hour. The band stopped playing and everyone counted down. Five, four, three, two…

"Happy New Year, baby doll," Jack whispered before kissing her.

"Happy New Year," Laura whispered. This happiness was sticking around a lot longer than a year.

Love and family lasted forever.

* * * * *

Dear Reader,

Thank you so much for picking up a copy of my first contemporary Christian romance. I hope you've enjoyed Jack and Laura's story. The idea seed for this book sprouted from a lasting image of a sad, old farmhouse I saw in the Upper Peninsula of Michigan. I have a major soft spot for old homes and often wonder what stories they hold.

Home and family are powerful themes that shape all of us. I don't think there's a family without their share of troubles, but God promises to be faithful to those who love Him. And trusting Him is the best decision any of us can make.

I'd love to hear from you. Please visit my Web site at: www.jennamindel.com or drop me a note c/o Steeple Hill Books, 233 Broadway, Suite 1001, New York, NY 10279.

Jenna Mindel

QUESTIONS FOR DISCUSSION

1. Laura rushed home because of her mother's stroke, and the fear this might be her last chance to see her alive. What might have happened had Laura waited until after her important dinner meeting?

2. Jack's prayer for help in finding a new place to live coincided with spotting the Toivo property for sale minutes later. Do you think God works through coincidences? Or does God make the coincidence? Either way, consider an example in your life where looking back you know God had His hand in the outcome.

3. Laura's drive for success stems from a childhood feeling that she never measured up to her mother's expectations. What drives you to excel?

4. Jack took drastic measures by uprooting his teenage daughter and moving north so he could build a solid relationship with her. What other ways might he have tried to reach her?

5. Laura believed in a general sense of God. She struggled with releasing her self-control to trust in Him. What does trusting God mean to you?

6. Jack says that he'd been consumed by his calling of veterinary medicine to the point of neglecting his family. He recognized the same workaholic tendencies in Laura. With today's demanding work schedules, how can a person maintain balance in their lives?

7. Laura held on to her hurt from the issues with her mother. Jack asked her to give the pain away to God and allow forgiveness to take over. What steps can a person take to offer up their pain to God?

8. Laura and her mother allowed deep-rooted insecurities to hold them back from experiencing life to the fullest. God calls us to be fearless because He is with us. Is there anything holding you back from fulfilling your dreams?

9. Jack and Laura's relationship progresses quickly. Is there an appropriate time frame for falling in love? Why or why not?

10. Laura comes to realize that family lasts forever. What threatens today's families? What makes them stronger? Take a moment to pray for your family.

*Scandal surrounds Rebecca Gunderson after she
shares a storm cellar during a deadly
tornado with Pete Benjamin.
No one believes the time she spent with
him was totally innocent.
Can Pete protect her reputation?*

*Read on for a sneak peek of
HEARTLAND WEDDING by Renee Ryan,
Book 2 in the AFTER THE STORM:
THE FOUNDING YEARS series
available February 2010
from Love Inspired Historical.*

"Marry me," Pete demanded, realizing his mistake as the words left his mouth. He hadn't asked her. He'd told her.

He tried to rectify his insensitive act but Rebecca was already speaking over him. "Why are you willing to spend the rest of your life married to a woman you hardly know?"

"Because it's the right thing to do," he said.

Angling her head, she caught her bottom lip between her teeth and then did something utterly remarkable. She smoothed her fingertips across his forehead. "As sweet as I think your gesture is, you don't have to save me."

A pleasant warmth settled over him at her touch, leaving him oddly disoriented. "Yes, I do."

She dropped her hand to her side. "I don't mind what others say about me. You and I, *we,* know the truth."

Pete caught her hand in his, and turned it over in his palm. "I told Matilda Johnson we were getting married."

She snatched her hand free. "You…you…*what?*"

He spoke more slowly this time. "I told her we were getting married."

She did *not* like his answer. That much was made clear by her scowl. "You shouldn't have done that."

"She was blaming you for luring me into my own storm cellar."

The color leached out of Rebecca's cheeks as she sank into a nearby chair. "I…I simply don't know what to say."

"Say yes. Mrs. Johnson is a bully. Our marriage will silence her. I'll speak with the pastor today and—"

"No."

"—schedule the ceremony at once." His words came to a halt. "What did you say?"

"I said, no." She rose cautiously, her palms flat on her thighs as though to brace herself. "I won't marry you."

"You're turning me down? After everything that's happened today?"

"No. I mean, *yes.* I'm turning you down."

"Your reputation—"

"Is my concern, not yours."

She sniffed, rather loudly, but she didn't give in to her emotions. Oh, she blinked. And blinked. And *blinked.* But no tears spilled from her eyes.

Pete pulled in a hard breath. He'd never been more baffled by a woman. "We were both in my storm cellar," he reminded her through a painfully tight jaw. "That means we share the burden of the consequences equally."

Blink, blink, blink. "My decision is final."

"So is mine. We'll be married by the end of the day."

Her breathing quickened to short, hard pants. And then…*at last*…it happened. One lone tear slipped from her eye.

"Rebecca, please," he whispered, knowing his soft manner came too late.

"No." She wrapped her dignity around her like a coat of iron-clad armor. "We have nothing more to say to each other."

Just as another tear plopped onto the toe of her shoe, she turned and rushed out of the kitchen.

Stunned, Pete stared at the empty space she'd occupied. "That," he said to himself, "could have gone better."

Will Pete be able to change Rebecca's mind
and salvage her reputation?
Find out in HEARTLAND WEDDING
available in February 2010
only from Love Inspired Historical.

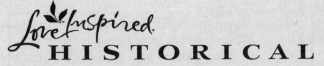

Love Inspired
HISTORICAL
INSPIRATIONAL HISTORICAL ROMANCE

After taking shelter from a deadly tornado, Rebecca Gundersen finds herself at the center of a new storm—gossip. She says the time she spent in the storm cellar with Pete Benjamin was totally innocent, but no one believes her. Marriage is the only way to save her reputation....

AFTER *the* **STORM**
The Founding Years

Look for

Heartland Wedding

by

RENEE RYAN

Steeple
Hill®

LARGER-PRINT BOOKS!

**GET 2 FREE
LARGER-PRINT NOVELS**
Love Inspired
**PLUS 2 FREE
MYSTERY GIFTS**

Larger-print novels are now available...

LILP10

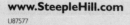